Eight in Three Weeks

and other early stories

Eight in Three Weeks
and other early stories

David Pablo Cohn

MONTEMAYOR PRESS
MONTPELIER, VERMONT

For more information contact:

Montemayor Press, P.O. Box 546, Montpelier, Vermont 05675
www.montemayorpress.com

Library of Congress Cataloging-in-Publication Data

Names: Cohn, David Pablo, 1963- author.
Title: Eight in three weeks : and other early stories / David Pablo Cohn.
Description: First edition l Montpelier, Vt. : Montemayor Press, 2017.
Identifiers: LCCN 2016057878 (print) l LCCN 2017014695 (ebook) l ISBN
  9781932727234 (paperback) l ISBN 193272723X (paperback) l ISBN
  9781932727227 (pbk. : alk. paper) l ISBN 1932727221 (pbk. : alk. paper)
Subjects: LCSH: Life change events--Fiction.
Classification: LCC PS3603.O3895 (ebook) l LCC PS3603.O3895 A6 2017 (print)
  l DDC 813/.6--dc23
LC record available at https://lccn.loc.gov/2016057878

For my mother Tamara and my sister Joanne,
who always seem to have time for a story

Eight in Three Weeks

and other early stories

Contents

The Duchess — 1

Abraham and Sarah — 15

Bragging Rights — 27

Tales From the Ice — 39

Coalinga, Northbound — 61

Everybody Has a Plan — 73

On Ziahtown Road — 83

Fly Away — 107

Jaguar — 115

Last Night Ashore — 125

The Coal Creek Quarterly — 137

The Slightest Trace of Gray — 157

Artifacts — 165

Water on Travertine — 183

Wenatchee, Last July — 191

Eight in Three Weeks — 205

The Duchess

No one was willing to say for sure whether Billy Eriksen's body was in the boat when they set it afire that night. I suppose it's better that way: any sort of certainty one way or the other would have raised uncomfortable questions about the disposal of human remains. And those noncommittal "Hmms" from the boys down at the shipyard seemed to give everyone enough leeway to believe that things had been resolved in a way Billy would have appreciated.

He'd been working on the *Duchess* for probably twenty years by then. His father had grown up working the mill, and when Billy finished his four years in Pullman, he returned to the peninsula with a Bachelor's degree in land management and a passion for cartography.

He took a job with the county and a bride from his graduating class at Chimacum High School. It wasn't that Susan Miller had been waiting for him, not exactly. It was just that over the years they'd been told by enough friends that they were well-suited to each other that, when the time came for their cohort to begin pairing up and breeding the next generation of Washingtonians, marrying seemed like the path of least resistance. With her parents' help, they bought a three-bedroom rambler off Sheridan Street and settled into their expectations.

It was hard to say when the troubles started. But their expectations had seemed to include a clutch of little Eriksens running rampant through the house, and as their neighbors' lawns bloomed with swing sets and wading pools, Billy and Susan's lack of offspring increasingly loomed as an uncomfortable gulf around which conversation navigated during neighborhood backyard barbecues.

To be fair, it wasn't as though they had greater troubles than other couples. But children have a way of stripping away the ambivalence in any marriage, either galvanizing a union or tearing it apart. Without that clarifying effect, Billy and Susan's marriage drifted into the shoals of quiet desperation. Doctors visits, couples counseling - even a six-month dabble with Tibetan fertility enhancement - nothing seemed to make a difference. And the more they attended to "the problem," the more it seemed to magnify the realization that theirs was to be an empty nest.

Susan filled her half of that emptiness by devoting herself to the city's children, earning a teaching certificate through the State Extension and taking on Social Studies for Grant Elementary. Billy filled his with a boat.

In retrospect, Billy's nautical turn surprised no one. Talk was always about boats around the counter down at the Blue Moose, and joining in that talk afforded him a rare conversational outlet that wasn't prone to veering off into laments about incomplete homework assignments or reflections on the moral character of tee-ball umpires.

The Moose was a local haunt, tucked around an improbable corner in the city boatyard, and somehow, early on, Billy and Susan had acquired the habit of heading down there Sunday mornings to split a stack of blueberry buttermilk pancakes and linger in the eavesdropped chatter. They were quickly welcomed as regulars, and before long Billy had picked up enough terminology to ask convincingly about the advantages of monofilament over nylon line, or how the co-op was planning to rig that new sloop of theirs.

The Sunday conversations did seem to placate Billy's restlessness, but also left him intoxicated in a way that made Susan wary: his normally attentive responses to her own musings about glitter and glue sticks always sounded farther away on the drive home, as he rode a broad reach to some foreign shore in his mind.

Of course he knew better than to talk about travel with Susan. There was money enough for indulgences, but aside from the honeymoon in Victoria and an uncle's funeral in Missoula, neither had even left Washington for more than a dip across the state line. The Millers stuck close to home, and Susan's domesticity prevailed on the Eriksen household as well: exotic destinations were best viewed after dinner on the Discovery Channel from the shared comfort of their Costco living room set.

So maybe conversation at the Moose just stirred that last trace of Viking blood in Billy's veins. Susan saw it coming, and when he came home one night with blueprints for a coastal cruiser, she consoled herself that the competition for his affections would only be a wooden boat, not a younger woman.

Besides, there was little real danger in the undertaking. Billy had sought refuge in plenty of other projects over the years. The guitar from Crossroads still hung on its hook in the living room, forlorn and resigned to a destiny as wall art. Golf clubs lasted two seasons before the financial mathematics of green fees saw them off on Craigslist. They were followed in uneven succession by birdwatching, bicycling, painting, and pottery.

His father's power tools, an antique bandsaw, table saw, drill press and entirely serviceable planer had gathered dust since the old man's sight failed, and he was happy for the promise that his wayward son might, however belatedly, take to the holy art of woodworking. It took three trips from the old Eriksen household to outfit Billy'd garage with the equipment necessary for building a boat.

But the enthusiasm that Billy's father held for his son's new obsession was shorter-lived than either of them would have liked. Old Man Eriksen - even his wife called him that - came from farming stock, and his love for woodcraft was strictly pragmatic. He saw it as a blessing to be able to fashion whatever useful implement he needed out of scrap lumber. A boat, by his reckoning, did not fit into any reasonable definition he could summon for the word "useful."

Still, he was happy to indulge his son; if nothing else, it was a chance to bond over the smell of sawdust and shouted conversation.

Billy chose the Seabird, a 25 foot carvel-planked yawl, as the vessel to carry his dreams. It had classic lines and an impeccable pedigree. That it was intended "for the amateur builder" was almost an afterthought for Billy; what had really captured his attention was an old black and white photo of Thomas Fleming Day reclining against the mast of the original

Seabird in the Azores, halfway across the Atlantic on his record-setting Providence-to-Rome run. Rome. The Azores. These were faraway names from the glowing screen of the Discovery Channel. And yet for $75, the mail order plans held some implicit promise of making Billy as intimately familiar with them as he was with the County Planning Office, or the Hilltop Tavern. Some days, on the drive home after a particularly unrewarding day at the County, he caught himself saying things, just to hear the sound of the words in his own voice: "You know, the last time we stopped in the Azores, we had to wait out Hurricane Martha. Started drinking Maracujá, and got ourselves kicked out of damned near every bar in Ponta Delgado."

He offered to call her the *Lady Susan,* but his wife would have none of it. "It's bad enough that she's stealing you away from me every evening," she said. "Damned if I'm going to have her take my name, too."

"Would you rather I called her the *Lady Virginia?"* Ginny Gordon's predations had been the downfall of more than one marriage in the neighborhood, and her unsuccessful attempt on Billy still served as a touchstone to their mutual commitment.

So somehow he settled on *The Duchess.* And while dinners still began with the conventional how-was-your-day-dears, Billy's thoughts increasingly skipped without segue to the growing stack of sawn ribs and planking that crowded the garage.

"We'll be outfitting her with two-inch foam insulation in the cabin," he might tell Susan over yams and turkey casserole one night. "We don't want to be running the heater all night if we take her up to the

Aleuts." she appreciated the deliberate "we," but settled for little more than asking polite questions and nodding in considered agreement where appropriate. In her mind, Billy's dinner conversation veered somewhere between thinking aloud and offering some vague accounting of how his evening would be spent. It was, if nothing else, a welcome bridge to the silences that had of late gone unpunctuated except by the clank of fork and knife against Corelle ware.

The more time Billy spent poring over plans, the more it always seemed there was to do, and the more discoveries there were of other things that would have to be done first. Susan's discreet inquiry to the shipyard boys one Sunday drew knowing smiles. Ole from the Wooden Boat School combed at his great gray walrus mustache and looked somewhere past her shoulder with pale blue eyes. Perhaps it *would* take a while, he mused. Perhaps - and he paused here to take special care with his words - perhaps Billy had come to an early understanding of a truth that all men learn when they grow old enough: that only dreams yet unrealized are still perfect. And that some dreams, perhaps, were better left that way.

It was five years before Billy finally laid a keel for the *Duchess*, years taken up by as much time in the library researching exotic destinations as were spent in the garage, measuring, cutting, and finishing actual pieces of wood. He still seemed to live with one foot in another world, but as Susan's polite questions drifted from halyards to Hawaii, from baseboards to Bimini, a new warmth and intimacy glimmered around the dinner table at the Eriksen household.

The Duchess

Sundays they still went down to the Blue Moose. When Clara came by to refresh their coffee, she seemed to know better than to ask how the *Duchess* was progressing. Most often she would simply set off on the weather or summer ferry traffic.

If Billy didn't slip away from his seat to join the shipyard conversation at the counter, it wouldn't be long before a couple of the inveterates ambled over to the corner to perch on borrowed seats and check in on him. Perhaps it was a charity of sorts, but their eyes were always bright with unfeigned enthusiasm as he recounted each week's progress.

When time did come for the keel, it took no one by surprise that floor space in the Eriksen garage came up three feet short. So the next summer was spent constructing a zinc-roofed longhouse sort of shed diagonally across the back yard, shadowed in the lee of a pair of white oaks that bordered their property to the south. That project, at least, went quickly: by September the shed had hanging lights, a radiant heater, portable stereo, and a second-hand couch where Billy could rest while contemplating the next step of his greater adventure.

They held an end-of-summer barbecue to christen the longhouse, Susan feeling for once an inexplicable lack of embarrassment over the absence of child-proofing around the yard. By then most of the remaining neighborhood children - those who hadn't gotten shopped out to grandparents or hauled back to Spokane when a husband strayed - were past the need for latch guards. It felt, if anything, like a coming out of sorts.

* * *

The *Duchess* was half-skinned when a January storm split one of the oaks, bringing a limb down through the longhouse roof. There was no visible damage, but the three weeks of intermittent rain that followed necessitated wrapping everything in plastic tarps to keep water off the untreated wood. By March, when he'd finally managed to secure the shed to his satisfaction, Billy ran his fingers over the *Duchess'* carvel seams with the tentative caress of a lover who suspected his mistress has been untrue. He broke the news to Susan over dinner.

"I'm just worried something's been compromised." Since there was no way to know for sure, he pulled all the planks off and set about re-skinning her from the keel on up. Susan offered no complaint and asked no questions.

It was the heart attack that changed everything. He'd left her voicemail Thursday afternoon saying he wasn't feeling particularly well and might be coming home early. By the time class got out, there were two more messages on her phone, a short, inaudible one from Billy, and one from Jefferson Healthcare saying her husband was resting comfortably, but would she please call the following number as soon as possible?

As far as heart attacks go, it was a good one, if such a thing existed: partial blockage of the left descending coronary artery, exacerbated by vascular spasms. The doctors were against surgery - blood thinners, Lotensin and a change of lifestyle, in their opinion, offered a better prognosis for long-term recovery.

Still, it was close to a year before his strength had returned enough for him to totter out over to the longhouse after dinner. Once it had, work on the *Duchess* resumed with a new passion. Dinners shrank first to an abbreviated affair, then quickly to a simple drive-by pass at the table as he carried his plate out to pore over hardware catalogs and cleat arrangements. Susan objected at first, then resigned herself to following him out with her own plate, providing companionship and an audience for his musings between forkfuls of turkey lasagna.

He did submit to her insistence on the doctor-prescribed twice-weekly walks. Wednesday evenings they usually limited themselves to a stroll down to the lagoon, but weekends he allowed her to drive to North Beach and lead him through the thicket of brush along the ramparts of Fort Worden.

She preferred taking to the beach below the bluffs on their way back, reveling in its fine iron sand, sea glass and makeshift driftwood shelters. But she noticed that Billy invariably focused on the damp tide-washed track just ahead of his feet as they walked, only ever looking seaward in brief, reluctant glances. When he did, there was an apprehension in his eyes, one she imagined she might feel if her wayward glance had caught the attention of some fearful animal. It was only when they were back to the safety of Sheridan that his gaze rose again to the horizon and his words returned to dreams of sailing.

She never did ask him about that - to even pose the question seemed an intrusion on some inner world he was unready to share. Even if it weren't, she was not entirely convinced that there was anything to be gained by probing the inconsistency of his behavior. After all, he seemed happy, happier than he had been any time in their marriage before the boat. Or maybe he was just content - and at this stage in their lives, she wasn't sure there was that much practical difference between the two.

The night that it happened, the night his heart gave out for good, she found him seated in the cockpit, reclining against the starboard coaming like he was just pausing to catch his breath. The corner chisel lay on deck just below his hand, a faint V-shaped divot marking the end of its brief flight.

There had been some late nights these past few months, and over the years she'd gone to bed alone more than once. Most times he would join her by midnight, floorboards creaking against the futility of his tiptoed approach. There would be a whispered apology, and he'd slide across to rest his arm against the curve of her gently rising back. But more than once she'd woken alone, too, and found him dozing out in the longhouse, sprawled across the couch and snoring amid crumpled advertisements for self-tailing winches.

That night, the night it happened, she'd gone out to tell him she wasn't going to wait up. There would be projects to grade tomorrow, and she needed her full eight hours if she wasn't going to be caught face down and drooling on the break table in the teachers' lounge.

It wasn't unusual for the longhouse to be quiet - she knocked on the door and called Billy's name before entering - best not to startle him in the middle of some delicate operation. But the moment she saw the angle of his head, lolled back like that and gaping open-mouthed at the ceiling, she knew.

The funeral was to be a small, neighborhood affair. Billy's living only kin by that time was an estranged brother somewhere in the South, so Susan's family, as usual, stepped into the breach and made the necessary arrangements. There was a memorial service at Grace Lutheran. Billy's manager at the County delivered the eulogy, followed by short reminiscences from Susan's brother, a couple of coworkers and a smattering of the neighborhood dads.

It wasn't until we saw them in the back two rows, squirming in unaccustomed Sunday neckties, that anyone thought to include the shipyard boys. They came forward to pay their silent respects afterwards, but it was hard not to feel that there had been a slight, and not only in the order of the service. Not one of the half-dozen speakers had failed to touch on the boat, if only in passing. Each had done so playfully, as comic relief against the litany of Billy's virtues: Billy was loyal, Billy was hard working, Billy was honest. Then, of course, there was the boat. That a man such as Billy should distract himself by building a boat seemed in their eyes to be a quirk, verging on character flaw; something that could only be rendered inert by dismissing it as an endearing eccentricity.

It was Ole who broached the question of what was to become of the *Duchess*. He approached Susan's brother during the reception, saying he hoped he wasn't being disrespectful. But her brother said it would be a kindness for him to call on her, so he did.

She led Ole through the house with a distracted welcome, opened the door to the shed for him, then stepped back, as if what lay within was a space where she no longer wished, or could bear, to set foot. He found her back in the kitchen when he emerged ten minutes later. It had taken only a glance to see that the boat was worthless, a well-intentioned but careless accumulation of tiny errors that would require far more time and money to correct than the collection of parts would fetch as scrap. But decency required that he remain there at least a little longer, if only to pay as much respect to the relic of a dead man's dream as to the man himself.

Susan's eyes flitted between the countertop and Ole's thoughtful scowl; at the very least, she must have suspected his conclusion, but could not bring herself to give words to the fear.

"I think we'll be able to find a good home for her."

He pursed his lips and nodded sagely with the pronouncement. Neither of them felt the need for elaboration, so she thanked him again and he excused himself to make arrangements.

The irregularities at the Wheelin Funeral Home came to light only in the week after the incident. The Millers maintained a family plot further down the peninsula, and Susan assumed that they'd be buried there together when the time came. But Old Man Eriksen had made it clear that he and his wife wished to be cremated when they passed on, and Susan's family saw no need to go against an Eriksen tradition of Nordic frugality.

In the aftermath, Susan admitted that she'd never really had a clear plan of what to do with Billy's ashes anyway, even if they hadn't been misplaced by the funeral home. Keeping an urn on the mantle always struck her as a little morbid. But the point was moot. And as the paper trail unraveled and it grew increasingly unclear whether Billy's body had even been delivered to the crematorium, it became impossible not to speculate on some connection between the missing remains and what happened off Boat Haven in the pre-dawn fog that following Thursday.

In retrospect, perhaps the most surprising part of it all was that the *Duchess* did, in fact, float. Ole had left her hull on a borrowed trailer in the shipyard's back lot pending some long-term plan. There seemed to be no point in securing either against the improbabilities of theft, so anyone with a two-inch hitch on their pickup could have backed her down the public ramp and hauled her clear of the jetty with shore lines. From there, the receding tide would have taken care of everything else.

The first report of fire was a call from the front desk at the Tides Inn: a somnambulant guest had observed an inexplicable orange glow flickering offshore in the fog. By the time the Coast Guard mustered a cutter, the *Duchess* was full ablaze in the bay, flames funneling and curling from the waterline up like an immense maritime bonfire.

The Navy also launched a rescue craft from Indian Island, and the two boats circled the drifting pyre as the current carried it seaward. There were ship-to-shore calls and requests for clarification, but in the end, a decision percolated up through the command chain to simply monitor the situation and let things run their natural course.

She eventually sank in 35 fathoms, just shy of the southbound shipping lanes. There was no flotsam to speak of, and within minutes not even a greasy stain remained to mark where the *Duchess* had ended her maiden and final voyage.

Of course the sheriff was called in to cordon the boatyard off as a crime scene. But there were no witnesses and few clues - the perpetrators had been so thoughtful as to hose the borrowed trailer clean of saltwater and return it to long-term parking. Buoyed only by the halfhearted charge of criminal mischief, the case itself quickly sank beneath a sea of more pressing investigations.

Susan still goes down to the Blue Moose most Sundays. The shipyard boys always stop by her corner to say hello, and Clara somehow makes time between the crush of other customers to linger and catch up over a coffee refill. She doesn't even ask before firing Susan's order off to Maggie behind the counter. Pancakes, of course. With blueberries, but also with something else, something liminal and tasting of far away. Those who claim to be versed in such things say it's Maracujá.

Abraham and Sarah

Honestly, there's no point in arguing who was responsible for the Abraham do-over. There was a lot going on then and frankly, I don't think there's anything to be gained by pointing fingers. I mean hey, the big guy commands Abe to sacrifice his son and then—ahem—at the last minute it's our job to let him know that it's just a test? Speaking as a humble messenger boy, I'd argue that there might be room for improvement in the corporate communications policy. As I said, I don't think there's anything to be gained by pointing fingers—all I know is that we had to call a do-over.

To be fair, that sort of thing is rare. Most of the time the angel gig is pretty sweet: a lot of the work is seasonal, and more often than not we spend our days bored out of our sweet little haloed heads, sitting around the great alabaster dispatch room in the sky and waiting for proclamations.

Every once in a while something pops out of the pneumatic and one of us has to scamper off to give the word to Noah or Ezekiel or Rosie Ortega on East 34th in Brooklyn. Yup, a cosmic singing telegram service, that's us. And yes, it's really a pneumatic—just like from those office buildings in the thirties. God knows whose idea that was—and you know I mean that literally. Really - we've got big white desks, swiveling office chairs with squeaky wheel casters and everything else you'd expect from a vintage newsroom. Think *His Girl Friday*, all done up in marble and alabaster.

I'm sure it wasn't always like that—at least I hope it wasn't. Something probably just caught his eye about the period. Or more likely, he proclaimed, "I hear the dispatch room's getting a little tired—Thou shalt spruce it up a bit." And whoever ran with it had a thing for Cary Grant.

Oh, and in case you're wondering—yeah, those are the sorts of proclamations we get: *"Spruce it up a bit,"* or *"Tell Samson to smite the Philistines"*—there's often not a lot of detail, so we have to wing it a bit. Heh. "Wing it"—we really do say that.

Sometimes though, we get a real doozy—you know the one about *"Remember to forget Amalek"*? I mean, you've got to believe the big guy was a little distracted when he dropped that into the tube. Maybe he'd been spending a little too much time on the Zen range, listening to trees falling in the forest and clapping with one hand. Or could be he was just yanking our chain—everybody's got to have a little fun, and I suppose you can get bored being omnipotent.

Anyhow, the Abraham do-over was a classic. The big guy decided he wanted to deliver a message himself and told Abe to "take your only son up to Mount Moriah" (Dude—what about Ishmael? Don't you keep notes?) and turn him into a barbecue offering. I'm sure he had it all worked out, but maybe he was on the celestial loo when Isaac was on the rock and the knife was out. We got word at the last minute (pop! goes the pneumatic) and had to skedaddle down and call the whole thing off for him.

Apparently we weren't quite quick enough: Abe thought God was doing a last-minute psyche out on him and went right ahead. Thwack. Goes without saying that the big guy wasn't happy, but no one was going to call him on sloppy direction.

So we asked for a do-over, rewound it a bit, and got to Abe a little earlier the second time around. Cued the Booming Voice—"Beeeep! This has been a test of the Emergency Sacrifice System. Had this been an actual sacrifice, you would have been provided with (poof!) a suitable ram caught in the thicket to use in your son's place."

Problem solved. Sort of—but you do know what happened with Sarah when he came back down off the mountain, don't you? Think about it: what would you do if your husband took your only son uphill with the sacrificial knife? Yup: keeled right over from a heart attack. And who could blame her?

Abe felt pretty bad about that. Everyone did—I don't think any of us saw that coming. I tell you, Gabe sat in a corner and moped for a week, and Azrael just said, "I don't want to talk about it," if you even looked like you were going to say anything. But no one was going to ask for a second do-over—we'd used our quota, and the big guy was not in a mood for arguing.

Which reminds me what I wanted to tell you about in the first place. I wanted to tell you about the other Sarah. Sarah Kaplansky, and her husband Abe. Yeah, Abraham and Sarah—their friends always thought that was cute. She liked to joke about never leaving him alone with the kids. Which was also cute because they didn't have any actual kids, and unless the big guy was going to do another gig with three angels coming down and making promises, they weren't going to have any.

"My music," she'd say. "My suites, my symphonies —those are my children." If she were feeling particularly sly, she'd add a bit about how many times Abe had already murdered them. They teased each other—constantly—but it was out of love.

Abraham was the son of a Polish bricklayer and a self-taught virtuoso on violin. Sarah was the daughter of a New York publisher, eager to escape the stifling expectations of Manhattan's upper crust. They met as teenagers in Boston, at the New England Conservatory. His father had spent half a week's wages on the train fare for his audition, and she'd convinced her own father that the program was a finishing school that would prepare her for her place in proper society.

It was love at first sight that morning in Jordan Hall —no, before first sight: she'd caught him improvising over one of her early compositions in the next room over. They'd played back and forth through the thin walls that morning, a musical inquiry, a conversation in A minor. Before they had even seen each others' faces, Abraham and Sarah knew they'd each found their match.

They soon became inseparable—each morning he would wait for her outside on Gainsborough and they'd walk to class together. It was predictable that life would be hard for them. Sarah's father refused to help, and Abe's father could give them nothing but his blessings. She brought in a little extra money as a composition tutor and he took on students of his own —he wasn't a gifted teacher, but he was patient and kind, and his skill with the violin brought money from parents who wanted their children to learn "from the best."

I tell you, it was lovely to watch those two—even back then we knew there was something special about them. Some evenings Gabriel would show up late, and we'd know he'd been perching in the arched windows at the back of the recital hall, listening as they coached and coaxed the best out of each other. "No, no, breathe it out on three, let it linger—oh yes, that's wonderful."

On Sundays they made a ritual of taking the T to Brookline. Rain, snow or shine they would buy sandwiches at Sharp's Deli and walk around the reservoir. They talked about the future, and Abe always asked Sarah to marry him. And she always said, "not yet"—not until she could support him in a manner befitting his musical genius.

It was two years later that she received her first commission—a small grant to write background music for a WGBH program on the American West. They celebrated with dinner in the North End, complete with fancy coffee drinks and dessert at Caffe Vittorio. That evening she said "yes," and the next morning they put a deposit on a one-bedroom apartment across the river in Cambridge.

Of course, her work is legendary now—I'm not ashamed to admit that we've cribbed a few bars up here from the Northern Suite and her Salome Trilogy for our heavenly chorus. And once Abraham secured a coveted seat in the Boston Symphony Orchestra, he demonstrated that he could bring her music alive like no one else. They became classical music's golden couple and found themselves reluctantly globetrotting for command performances—Westminster, Beijing, Dubai and the like. Neither of them looked particularly comfortable in the spotlight—both were homebodies, and you could tell they wore their concert dress with the resentment of sullen children at a fancy party. But travel and the spotlight were part of the package. Abraham's father lived long enough to see his son play Carnegie Hall and wept during the encore. Sarah's father showed approval in his own reserved way, commissioning her to write a piece for violin, to be played by Abraham at her younger sister's wedding.

Sarah retired—twice—unsuccessfully, each time coming back with a symphony that broke new ground in the orchestral world. Kaplansky's Third (in A minor of course), told the story of their courtship, mixing Old World melodies with the straight lines of a Manhattan sensibility. Her Fourth, in C major, evoked Italy from Etruscan times through the Roman Empire, the Dark Ages and into the Renaissance. She refused a commission from the Italian Consul for a sequel to bring the country up to date, saying the symphony had written itself—how could she create something that didn't come of its own free will?

After her Fifth (in A major, in honor of Beethoven's Seventh) Sarah disappeared from public life. Abraham continued to play, but would only travel reluctantly when the Symphony was on tour. He returned to Cambridge at every chance like a nervous mother with a child sick at home. No, there was nothing wrong— her health was fine. But she needed to concentrate. Yes, she was working—working very hard. So word spread and anticipation grew, like the tension that rises in the air before a storm on a summer day. From time to time, you could catch Abraham absentmindedly playing a few notes, a slow and mournful melody, or a chirping, birdlike tune before catching himself and stopping, then looking over his shoulder to see if anyone had heard.

The thunderclap came unexpectedly, on a cold, wet November morning two years later. Sarah appeared at the desk of the orchestra's managing director, haggard, bleary-eyed and wearing summer clothes, as though she'd not thought to look outside before setting off. She was clearly not well. But all she said was, "Here. It's ready." She laid the manuscript on his desk and left.

Ozawa was the next person to know, followed by the board of directors. There was supposed to be a formal announcement, but of course by then word had gotten out and the musical world tripped over itself plunging into a frenzy of anticipation. Abraham rushed home from Moscow, leaving an understudy to take his place for the remainder of the week's run. Rehearsals were scheduled and musicians sworn to secrecy, further fueling the wild speculation.

The board decided that the Symphony would debut the piece on January 9th—Raphael put it on the calendar so we wouldn't forget. For lack of a better name, the press dubbed it Kaplansky's "New Year's Symphony," and I'll wager we weren't the only ones holding our collective breath to hear it.

Sarah was still sick when January brought the ragged edge of a Nor'easter to town. Lines were down everywhere and the streets were one big sheet of ice, but there was no way the Symphony was going to cancel. This was Kaplansky, after all, and these were Bostonians. They'd complain like hell about the weather, but then they'd throw on muck boots and trench coats over their tuxedos and make the trek, across Siberia if necessary, to hear Sarah Kaplansky's New Year's Symphony.

Upstairs, we were busy getting ourselves dolled up for the evening when "Fwoomp!"—out came another heavenly proclamation. We popped it out of the tube to pass around... and you could see the ice settle into each face as we absorbed the message. Like most, it was a short one. It just said:

"Sarah Kaplansky shall not live to hear the end of her symphony."

Now, most proclamations are To-Whom-It-May-Concern jobs, and we flip a coin for who goes. But none of us wanted to take this one. None of us. Really, it just wasn't fair. I mean, we do a lot of stuff that doesn't seem fair to folks on the ground, and that's okay—we know there's a plan. But this? There had to be a better way. Let her climb the steps to pick up her flowers on the stage. Take a bow, then boom and down, right in front of her adoring fans, ensuring the legend of Sarah Kaplansky forever. Sure, everybody's got to go, but it wouldn't be so bad like that, would it? But no—she wasn't even going to make it to the end of the show, and one of us had to be the one to take her out.

So there we were, standing around the alabaster dispatch desk: looking at each other, looking at the mortal proclamation. None of us were willing to touch it—what if none of us *did* take it?

The agony of the moment stretched on until, with another little whoosh of air, Azrael popped in, back from his Angel of Death rounds. He looked at us, looked at the table and said, "Oh hey—I've been waiting for this one." He snatched the proclamation up, stuffed it in his belt and Poof!—was gone again.

Well, from that point on, there wasn't a lot we could do except watch. So we watched. We hovered invisibly over the cheap seats and watched with dread and anticipation.

Sarah was sitting in A25 with her sister on her right. She still looked pretty awful, but at least someone had dressed her for the weather. Ozawa was directing, and boy, you had to admit he looked nervous—he kept glancing over his shoulder at Sarah while he was adjusting his stand. He must have known more than anyone else that this symphony would be a doozy.

The lights dimmed, the audience hushed and BLAM!—the opening *tutti* hit us like Stravinsky in a streetcar accident. When we peeled ourselves off the back wall, the woodwinds were playing a sinuous wandering melody that spoke of sand, of tents billowing in midday heat. And of a man wandering in the desert.

She was telling the story of Abraham. No, not her Abraham, but the first one. She told of going down to Egypt, of Lot and his wife, of Hagar, Ishmael, and the first covenant. The movements flowed together like water—there was no telling where one story ended and the next began. The instruments and themes took on lives of their own. By the fourth movement, there were no more flutes and kettle drums—there were angels and earthquakes. Sodom and Gomorrah had fallen in a blaze of brass fire, and the covenant sealed in a quiet meditation of the oboe. Then Isaac and the strings began their tortured climb up Mount Moriah and the musical tension climbed with them. This was where it was going to end—I couldn't watch, and I couldn't look away. At the summit, the clouds circled in the rumble of kettle drums. Ozawa was leaping, leaving the ground as he coaxed the woodwinds and strings into opposition, the argument, the binding. As the crescendo built, the violin in Abraham's hands was no longer a violin—it was a knife, poised to do the unthinkable.

And then? At the instant of the fatal blow, Abraham hesitated. At least I think he hesitated. There was a single gasp audible in the moment of silence, then a crash that could not have been made by any earthly instrument, and the entire hall plunged into darkness.

The audience went wild, leaping to their feet with cheers and whistles. But as the emergency lighting came up, it was clear we weren't through—the orchestra was still in position, frozen at attention while a single horn swayed gently in the rhythm of a high, quiet tune. The unheralded ram in the thicket, its call drowned out by the tumult of the crowd.

And then? Then it was really over. Ozawa turned and bowed, but the audience was already cheering as loudly as they could. The orchestra rose and a spotlight flicked to the front row. Sarah was being lifted from where she fell—half carried and half-led to the stage under a barrage of flowers.

Pneumonia took its toll in the following months of convalescence. Abraham was rarely far from her bedside as she recovered, and her hearing was badly damaged, leaving only the lower registers in one ear. "Everything above middle C sounds like a dog whistle now," she'd say. It didn't much affect her composing, but she swore off major works and contented herself with short pieces for friends. Her only regret, she said, was that with all the noise from the crowd on opening night, she never did get to hear the end of her last symphony.

It took a while to get up my nerve, but eventually I did ask Azrael about it. I mean, in any business you tend to stick with what you're good at, and he *is* the Angel of Death, right? So—big bolt of lightning? Sure. Quiet little aneurysm? Sure. But blowing a transformer at the Back Bay substation? That seemed like a bit of a departure.

He gave a sly, sideways kind of look around and lowered his voice. He said that, you know, sometimes the big guy doesn't want to let everyone in on a do-over. Not when he's the one who's called it. He might even pull someone in on the side—quiet-like, so no one else would even notice it happened.

"You've got to understand: he's still feeling bad about how it ended with the other Sarah—the first one. So this time? Maybe this time he wanted her to see that it turned out okay in the end."

Bragging Rights

I wanted that scar, damn it. I wanted to be able to strip my sleeve up to my shoulder when school started again and wave that contused, jagged line in front of all the other boys in fifth grade. I wanted to be able to say, in my best Chuck Yeager, "Aw, it's nothin', but let me tell you how it happened: There I was, at the top of the road into Rattlesnake Gulch, with fresh rain frozen over the old snow in the ruts left when the wranglers hauled their trailers out to the upper pasture. Just me and my Flexi-Flyer, and that road challenging us to take the ride of a lifetime."

That's what I wanted, at least.

There were a few problems with my plan, though, the least of which was that I was the only one in Ouray County who actually called it Rattlesnake Gulch. But I couldn't forget about that summer before, when Kenny Bunker fell out the back of his uncle's four-by on Dickerson Road. He was supposed to be keeping the hay bales held down, and I guess he wasn't minding the store. One started to go over the side after a bump and Kenny tried hanging on but went right over with it, bouncing around into the ditch and breaking his arm. So when school came around in September and he was swaggering around with his cast—well, I've got to admit that I felt a spot of something watching everyone nose up to him. Girls cooing like he was some damned war hero—hell, boys treating him like some damned war hero, too. Miss Jensen even said he could have Suzanne Kramer help with his writing, seeing as how it was his right arm that broke. If that was all right with Suzanne which, from the cooing, sounded like it was more than. I thought Really? Suzanne Kramer and a clown like Kenny Bunker? I'd show them.

I guess some things just make more sense when you're eleven.

I picked the day after New Year's for my fateful plummet. It was the Saturday before school got back, and I figured that, if I played it right, I could even miss a day or two while I was "recuperating." There was a good sheen of ice on the road. It hadn't snowed since my dad had made a trip up to the pasture to check on how the new fence was holding up, and the traces from his pickup ran the length of the hill like gently-interwoven lanes of a hick town bobsled course. Hell, looking at that track, I might have tried it even if I hadn't already gotten it in my head to have a go.

I swapped into my jeans and flannel as soon as we'd got home from Bible study and helped ourselves to lunch from the holiday leftovers. My mom was preoccupied with getting the house back into whatever semblance of order it'd had before Christmas, and Cindy was at the kitchen table, nose-deep in some science book the cousins gave her. Occasionally she'd call out to no one in particular, "Hey—did you know that the human body has ten times as many bacteria cells as it does human cells?" After a "What was that, dear?" my mother would nod and opine that there were plenty of things she was better off not knowing.

No one paid me any mind as I tromped by, casually as I could, to fetch my boots and bomber hat from the mud room.

"I'm going out sledding, Ma."

I was proud of that hat. Most kids around town wore those peaked, knit wool-and-polyester ski caps that you could pick up at the hardware store, but last year my father had returned from Denver with a genuine leather bomber hat for my birthday. It had big earflaps, a chin strap and a flip-up brim thick with real coyote fur. Putting that hat on made you somebody who could strut. It made you invincible. It gave you ideas.

Getting up the hill the first time required a bit more effort than I'd planned for. I could probably have managed the frozen tracks from my father's truck if I weren't also hauling the sled behind me, but the ice-cast tread from his tires didn't provide quite enough traction to counter the drag of the sled's runners. Abandoning the tracks meant wading through old knee-high snow that had crusted and gave way unevenly as I plodded through it. I fell twice on the way up, cursing as manfully as I could each time.

It was only when I reached the top, unexpectedly out of breath, that I discovered the first flaw in my plan. My father's round trip had left four separate tracks down the road, but no two of them were spaced quite right for the runners of a Flexi Flyer. There were some spots partway down the hill where his tracks merged and split; I was sure I could make a little headway there, but to what end? I'd set my mind on a brag, and it demanded I sled the whole damned hill, from crest down to where it petered out into Route 14.

I tried setting my sled down on the unbroken crust. It held a little, but immediately fell through up to the slats when I put any weight on it. Pushing with my knees and boots was an exercise in futility. I discovered I could balance myself with one runner in the track and one on the crust, but any forward motion dragged the sled sideways before I developed any speed, either sinking into the crust or flopping over, leaving me face up against the ice, contemplating a blue January sky.

Clearly, the Flexi Flyer was not going to work, and my thoughts turned to inner tubes, or one of the old cafeteria trays my mother had stacked in the garage for no apparent reason.

I was about a quarter way back down the hill when I came to a place where my father's two traverses had crossed over each other to clear a rut in the road. There was a section before and after the crossing where his tracks were close enough to get both rails of the sled on the hard pack. It wasn't a full run, not by any means, but it was something, at least, and it would save me a bit of walking with the sled unevenly dragging, then nipping at my heels.

I cinched my bomber on as convincingly as I could manage, wedged the tail of the runners into the uphill bit of crust, splayed my legs over the side of the sled and hunched forward over the steering bar. This close to the ground, a hill always looked steeper than it was.

Now, I hadn't, at that point, really put any thought into how I expected the run to end; I was already 20 yards downhill, gritting my teeth against the rising pitch of metal rails clattering on frozen tread when the question occurred to me.

But I wasn't worried, not in the least. I'd steeped too long in the American ideals of manly improvisation: I was a jet fighter, whipping through canyon lands at Mach 1 to outsmart those bogeys. Where the two tamped-down paths diverged at the first curve, I leaned heavily on the right runner and drove the left side hard into the foot-high crusted berm of snow. It exploded into a gratifying cloud of chunks and white powder, jolting me, blinding me, but not—apparently —slowing my downhill plunge.

The road veered to the right ahead; I remembered it from the endless summer hikes up to the pasture and could see, beyond the dripping and snow-drenched fur of my hat, where the line of old oaks formed the outside perimeter of the turn. Two paths crossed again, and I followed the inside line, briefly accelerating even more as both runners found ice.

This time, as the paths diverged, I took the junction head on and was rewarded by an even larger explosion of snow. Even better, at this speed (now somewhere past "exhilarating" and approaching "uncomfortable") I found myself skating on thin ice. My runners were now skittering over the crusted surface faster than they could break through it, and as the hill fell away into its second turn, my vision narrowed and muscled tensed in what I later learned were the classic initial symptoms associated with unmitigated panic.

By now I was no longer, in any practical sense, steering. The sled crested the road's crown where it reversed into another broad turn to follow the valley slope above Route 14 and I dropped fleetingly into another set of iced tracks. I was too terror-stricken to appreciate the "foom" of snow and ice as I hit the other side and left the road obliquely, though I do remember a glimpse of juniper, and gratitude at not hitting it head-on.

Then I was airborne. For a silent moment, the whole of the Ouray Valley lay before me, the slope dropping away as if in a fly-over movie sequence. My sled flew with me, Pegasus to my Bellerophon, my hands still tight on the steering bar.

But the vision lasted only a moment, and then the mesquite and ice and rocks rose up to smite us. I bounced once and thought, fleetingly, that I might just be able to stay on the sled. Then the earth was gone and there was sky above me. In the next instant, I was flayed from head to foot by mesquite, tearing at my head, my coat, my hands, and flung again into the hard slope, tumbling, bouncing like a rag doll until I had slowed enough for a juniper windbreak to arrest my descent.

I lay there with my eyes closed for a good five minutes, cradled in ice and branches like the Pietà, catching my breath and trying to recollect the events that had brought me there. As the cold began to seep through where my jeans met the snow, so did an awareness that I hurt. In a lot of places. I'd read somewhere about people snapping their necks and not knowing it until they tried to get up, so I started with my fingertips, wiggling them, then my whole hands and arms before trying to move my head and roll laboriously to hands and knees. In retrospect, if I had snapped my neck, my precautions would have done nothing to save me, but after the excitement of my arrival, perhaps something in my brain just needed an excuse to take things slowly.

By the time I'd managed to make it to my knees, I had a pretty good catalog of where I was damaged. Jeans were torn at the butt and on both knees, one of them bleeding a bit and stinging like the devil. One sleeve was ripped clear open, and it looked like I had a patch of road rash the size of my hand on the exposed shoulder. My back? Well, my old parka had taken the brunt of the impacts, but my muscles and bones felt like I'd been beaten head to tail with a hammer all the way. Which, given the incline I'd come down, wasn't far from fact.

It was only when I went to brush something out of my eye that I got worried. The side of my face above my cheek was sticky, and when I looked at my hand, the tips of my fingers were red and bright. Yup, I'd cut myself, alright, just on the outside edge of my left brow. I'd had worse, I suppose, but this one was bleeding plenty.

Panic seized me—what if I got blood on my hat? But my heart sank even as I reached to pull it clear: the beloved bomber was no longer on my head. Bits of ice still clung to my ear, and a gentle breeze ran through my matted, wet hair. I was on my feet in a second, damn the peril. Looking up the rocky, mesquite-covered slope, there was no trace of the hat, and very little of the path I'd taken on my way down.

Climbing back up felt like Everest. There was nothing resembling a trail over the rocks and snow, and every step seemed to reveal another bruise that I had sustained the first time I came this way. Between breaks to catch my breath and detours around impenetrable thickets (I had come through them on the way down, hadn't I?), it must have taken close to an hour to make my way back to where I'd left the road.

I found the sled not far from the top, where it stood embedded, tombstone-like in a drift, and hauled it up with me to the road. A pair of thin lines and the furrow of one dragged foot—too little, too late—disappeared at the edge of the precipice, commemorating the starting point of my ill-advised flight.

I was just about as beat up and tired as I'd ever been in my life, and the reflex of wiping my brow from the effort had left bloody streaks half the length of my left sleeve. But I stared down that incline where the tracks left off and knew I couldn't leave without my hat.

The sun was dropping toward Elk Ridge by the time I gave up. I'd made a second descent—on foot this time—beating at juniper scrub and scouring the mesquite for that patch of gray fur and brown leather, brilliantly and unintentionally camouflaged against the winter landscape. It was only when I reached the stand of trees that had caught me that I realized I'd left the sled up on the shoulder of the road above, far enough above that it was still in sunlight while I sulked in the shadow of the mountain ridge. I sat and cried then, the big, hot, unashamed tears of a man-child who has spent all he had and still come up short.

A survival instinct overtook me as it grew dark. Not that I was worried about freezing out there, but if I were gone long enough to make my mother wonder, there'd be no way I could sneak back in without getting pulled up by the ear for having ruined my jeans and winter coat.

I suppose I could have made up some tall tale about having gotten hit by a car, or falling off some precipice

—honestly, it wasn't all that far from the truth. But we'd had plenty of dinner table conversation about the difference between a convenient version of the truth and a bald-faced lie. And even on a good day, I wasn't about to lie to my folks.

It was full on night as I tiptoed up the side steps. Chatter from the kitchen and an empty front parlor told me dinner had not yet been rung; I called "I'm home!" from landing on my way up, grabbed a t-shirt and spare pair of jeans and ducked into the bathroom to survey the damage.

It wasn't pretty. The gash above my forehead was the only real cut, but it had bled profusely, and I'd managed to smear the sticky residue into my hair and across both cheeks. The jacket looked like a fine prop for some zombie movie, with one sleeve hanging loose and splotched with bloody handprints.

My efforts at washing made everything worse, as splashing water from the faucet left walls and floor around the sink speckled in streaky red. I mopped up as best as I could before retreating to the tub.

"You okay in there, son?"

Given my distaste for washing, the sound of the shower, just before dinner, had apparently raised some eyebrows downstairs.

"Yeah, fine! Fine." I tried not to sound too insistent —somehow, it was now enormously important that I not admit to having hurt myself.

"Okay…" There was, by my reckoning, a thoughtful pause. "Well, dinner's in five. And it's your turn to set."

I squeegeed the mirror and peered back into it once I'd dried off and rolled the now-ruined, blood-stained towel into my jeans and jacket to hide—somewhere. The forehead gash blended almost imperceptibly with the top of my eyebrow, and hot water had brought my lip down to the level of a pre-teen pout. There were some other scrapes, sure, but on the whole, I'd gotten off easy.

"Dinner, Jamie!"

Disposing of the evidence would have to wait.

"You have fun this afternoon, son?" It was meant as small talk.

"Yes, sir. Went sledding out on the road up to the pasture above 14."

He nodded, satisfied, and had half a word out of asking my sister the same before my mother spoke.

"Oh, Jamie—what happened?" She leaned forward over the table, a hand on my chin, turning my head so she could see. I'd been trying to sit sideways a little to keep my good side toward her and my father, but she seemed to know something was up.

"It's nothing, Mom."

"When did this happen?"

I knew she could see me thinking. "On the way home. I...I wasn't paying attention—ran into a tree."

I have no idea why I said it like that. It was the strangest sort of lie: true under only the most oblique examination, and told to no real proper end. I was saving myself from nothing.

"Well, let's get some Bactine on that right after dinner. Can't have it getting infected, can we?"

I sat patiently on the footstool while Cindy did the dishes. My mother dabbed the stinging Q-Tip across my forehead as though painting on a third eyebrow, then applied a layer of folded gauze and two curved strips of cloth tape to hold it in place. She stepped back to admire her handiwork.

"Well, you can just thank God you don't have class tomorrow."

I couldn't agree with her more: in the mirror I looked like a half-made-up circus clown with one giant, arched white eyebrow.

As it turned out, I didn't have class the following day, either. The fever came over me Monday night, and by morning I was sweating and shaking something awful. Dr. Olson diagnosed pneumonia and prescribed amoxicillin and bed rest.

It took a full week before I was steady enough on my feet to make it up the road to school. By then, the cut above my eyebrow had faded to nothing more than an uneven scab line, and no one in fifth grade had any interest in a piddling cut when they heard that I'd gotten to skip a whole week for pneumonia. Miss Jensen said it shouldn't take me that long to make up the missed work, seeing as how things always got started slowly in the new year. But she wrinkled her nose a little when I asked if Suzanne Kramer could help me, as if she didn't understand the question. She said she supposed that was up to Suzanne, wasn't it?

I told my mother that someone at school had swiped my jacket, and hid it along with the torn jeans and ruined towel out under some loose river rock on the bank of Canyon Creek. They were gone when I went by a few days later; taken by coyotes, I'd wager.

But the hat? Yeah, that's the point I was getting to: You see, I forgot all about the hat. It had never been a part of the original wager—not like the hill, not like the scar. Not like Suzanne Kramer. And I think it's the things we don't realize we're risking that are the hardest to lose. Maybe that's why we have phrases like "collateral damage": we need special words, and special ways of thinking to let us isolate ourselves from unexpected loss. To let us wall it away somewhere, so we don't have to confront it face to face. That's what I need you to remember. I loved that bomber, and it never occurred to me in a million years that I might lose it. But by the time I made it down the mountain that night, it was already a ghost. Next freeze, I think I just grabbed one of my dad's hardware store caps off the pegs in the mudroom and never looked back.

Suzanne married Kenny the summer after senior year. She's probably still out there, popping out little baby Bunkers like a dutiful farm wife. Honestly, I lost track of all that when we moved east.

The funniest thing is that I still have that damned sled somewhere. A January storm buried the upper pasture in two feet of snow, and it was well into the spring muck before I ventured up there again in rubber boots. My forlorn little Flexi-Flyer was still standing vigil where I'd left it at roadside, now half-buried in runoff with one gleaming runner pointed obliquely in the direction of my fateful plunge. I dragged it home lovelessly, trailing it behind me as my boots sucked at the mud, not even thinking to touch the faded keepsake line above my right brow.

Tales From the Ice

It didn't matter whether you had a story to tell or just wanted to sit back and listen to somebody else's tale of wonder and woe over a shot of bad whiskey: Summer Camp Lounge was the place to go for stories. "Summer Camp" was a story in itself, its name a laudably evocative euphemism for the scattered Jamesways that served as overflow housing for the station. It always felt like a little like the Wild West out there, an outpost of relative lawlessness a quarter mile downwind of the station proper. Management only tolerated it within the rigor of the Program because it seemed to help keep "bad" behavior concentrated into one easily contained location and, as such, they made a point of not venturing out uninvited. If pressed, Carter would simply espouse the unofficial view that it was best for everyone if what happened in Summer Camp stayed there.

The Lounge was just another dismal Jamesway—a diesel-heated canvas tent left over from the Korean War—set in the middle of the pack and filled with old furniture discarded from God knows where. At its center, like an altar, stood a cracked and stained wood veneer portable bar that must have come down during the bad old days as a "morale expense."

Most nights you could be pretty sure of finding Heller at the pulpit there, holding church for Team Testosterone. No, they weren't all ex-Navy, but enough of the guys had come through the service to create a sense of common culture.

"You know," Heller would loudly proclaim while dispensing a shot of whiskey from some dubious bottle of leftovers, "Back on the sub, people understood that there were expectations." "Here, here!" we'd all cry, though I suspect most of us had no idea what he was talking about.

"I mean, when a new guy came aboard, it was understood that he'd bring a dozen issues with him. *Penthouse* or *Hustler* or whatever, to pay his way. He'd hand them off to you and you'd give him all your old shit that you just couldn't stand to look at any more."

He'd pause for dramatic effect, and we'd wait breathlessly. Heller wasn't a particularly big man, but he was squarely built and had the preacher's gift for appearing larger than life when delivering fire and brimstone.

"These days, though?" He peered at the choir and picked out a victim. "Ross—what did you bring?"

We all liked Ross. That Iowa farm boy haircut betrayed him as within spitting distance of his teens, but he was an earnest kid, eager to learn, and quick to pitch in. And while, like me, he'd never been in the service, he was just as happy as anyone to be embraced by the fraternity.

"Nothing. I brought nothing, Heller." He raised his hands in mock surrender. "Hey, nobody ever told me!"

Heller passed judgment with a slam of his whiskey bottle gavel.

"That's exactly what I'm talking about: a breakdown in the social order!"

And we'd all cheer, and Heller would pour Ross another shot, and Captain Robby would start in on the story about last summer, when someone started leaving brown paper bags with old copies of Playboy in people's mail slots, signing himself the "Skua Santa."

"Hey, I don't mind a little fresh porn. It was just unnerving to be sitting there in the galley talking to Carter or Melinda, wondering if they were the one who just slipped you a spank mag...."

It was a gentle, affectionate hazing. Hell, we all remembered how hard it was being the FINGY, the fucking new guy, when you didn't know anyone, didn't know anything. It took a while to learn how things were done down here. It took a while to learn all the names, all the faces. It took damned near forever to learn all the stories.

Two years ago that had been me, wide-eyed and wondrous, gawking like I'd been dropped off on another planet and someone had forgotten to tell me the rules. They just let me wander around the South Freakin Pole—of the world, for god's sake—when I wasn't working on the diesels. Like it was an ordinary place, a place on earth, rather than, well, I don't really know what.

Sure, the wondrous things became ordinary after a little while, but somehow there were always more wondrous things to take their place. The way ice rainbows hung inverted and the sun slid counter-clockwise around a blue-gray sky. The way the snow creaked like Styrofoam beneath your boots, and your breath, on a clear day, made a little whooshing sound as it froze. Even deep within the Season of Pain, when we were all just counting the hours until we got to slog our bag out to the runway, out to the churning, throbbing Herc that would carry us home from this godforsaken moonbase. Even when our sleep was filled with dreams of forgotten places where the air was thick and sweet, where the earth itself was lush and green and alive. Even then I could step out into the waning sunlight of Antarctic dusk and lose myself in the wonder of it all.

Yeah, I was a lifer. Carter says you find out pretty quick, and I knew right away. Even before I'd finished my first season. Even before I knew that Audrey was gone. Maybe Audrey knew, too. Maybe that was why she left.

The Pole was still wondrous three years in. But I know we all had our moments, moments in the quiet lull, moments in the still-luminous small hours of the night when the pain snuck through. Carter sat down with me one afternoon, early in that first season, while I was perched out on the deck at Alpha. Just sat down next to me without any words and looked out across the blowing snow with those ancient pale blue eyes. We watched for a minute or so before he spoke.

"You know, Drew, being out on the ice will make you feel more liberated than you've ever felt in your life." He shook his head, slowly. "Also more lonely." Three years in, I still don't know if he meant that as comfort or a prediction.

I think it hits all of us at some point, and when it does, you have a couple of choices. Some folks like to throw on their bunny boots and parka and stroll out to the End of the World. Standing there at the edge of this insignificant fleck of humanity, gazing downwind across a thousand miles of breathless ice desert is always a good reminder of just where your stupid little misery stands in the grand scheme of things.

The End of the World is a fine place for perspective, but sometimes the clarity of its message is a little too severe. Sometimes you need softer medicine; when you do, you head to Summer Camp Lounge. You head there to minister to your wounds with alcohol and camaraderie. To seek solace and sympathy from your fellow misfits. You head there to hear stories, stories that remind you that yes, you are an irrelevant speck floating in the cosmos, but for now, at least, you have company along for the ride.

Today had been one of those days, and I knew what I needed as I pushed my way in through the door, plunging from eternal, incandescent glare into the warm, smoky comfort of the ancient canvas womb. Company. Escape. Oblivion. Or maybe just another story, like the one about when Storm's tractor fell through the ice into the old, buried station, 40 feet down. And how they lost another tractor trying to pull it out before just deciding that the whole damned area was off limits.

But there were different voices coming from the bar tonight; not Heller, but four, no, three women, all hunkered around a clatter of bottles. Alex, Maura, and another voice, husky and familiar. I squinted down the darkened half-pipe of the Lounge and tried to make out faces.

Alex saw me first. "Drew? Sweetie! Come on over and join us for a drink."

Maybe the End of the World would have been a better bet. Alex called everybody "sweetie," but it was still enough to pull at your heart a little. Precisely the kind of pull I didn't need tonight. Yeah, Alex was that all-American girl we'd grown up dreaming about: beautiful, blonde, busty. Not that she abused her gifts; if anything, they seemed to fill her with some sense of obligation to share. Somehow she managed to make everyone feel special, grateful for that wink across the galley, or that brief tousle of hair as she passed in the corridor.

But no, not tonight—I didn't think I could handle those kinds of endearments. I balked and turned back to the door. Someone, years ago, had hung a sign there proclaiming the tent "Nate's Fight Club." I'd been meaning to get the story behind that. Like I said, there are a hell of a lot of stories down here.

The third voice bellowed out at me. "Oh come on, you wanker. I'm flying out in the morning. Least you can do is send me off."

Kathy. Right. One of the electricians, probably a dozen years my senior, with close-cut, gray speckled hair and eyes the color of a winter sky. She looked like she was born wearing Carhartts and a tool belt. Usually played the strong, silent type, but I'd seen her hold court too, quietly taking in kids who couldn't stomach the Navy crowd.

I surrendered my prospect of escape and advanced down the halfpipe. "Your contract's up already?"

"Nope." There was a trace of self-satisfaction in her voice. "Got a better offer up in Fairbanks."

"So you're just leaving us?"

She tucked her thumbs smugly into the bib of her Carhartts and leaned back, Farmer John feigning modesty over his prize-winning pumpkin. "A girl's gotta do what a girl's gotta do."

I knew that, technically, we could quit any time. But I'd never known anyone to actually just do it. At least, not without serious cause. Like their kid back home got sick, or they couldn't hack the cold. Or their wife... I let the thought escape, unpursued.

Kathy didn't see any problem. She'd told her sup when the offer came in and said she'd like to give notice. Electricians were always in demand on the ice, so he asked if she'd be willing to wait until he could get a replacement on site. She said yes, and they worked out a deal where he signed her off as contract complete for staying on a couple more weeks. Even got her a quarter of her end-of-season bonus.

"For bailing on your contract?"

"Hey, you work with them, they'll work with you. Especially if you're bailing on your contract." She gave a little snort and snatched up the bottle of Jameson's, flourishing it like a saber before topping off the half-full tumbler on the counter at her hip. "They're legally obligated to get your sorry ass back home no matter how you quit. But you'd be surprised how much latitude they have in how they do it." She snorted again. "And what counts as home."

Turns out they'd even had people quit mid-winter, when no one could get in or out for nine months.

"Henry was your year, right, Maura?" Kathy threw the name down like a wager.

Maura was tucked over the bar, clasping an oversized plastic Power Rangers mug to her chest. She rolled her eyes, as if even the thought of Henry made her dizzy. "Hellllllll, yeah. First week in July. Fine one day, full-on toasty the next."

She saw me doing the math in my head and saved me the trouble.

"Four fucking months. Four fucking months until the first flights came in and we could get his ass out of here. Four fucking months watching him wander around the station like a ghost. He'd show up at mealtimes, grab a plate of food and disappear back into his room. If you ran into him in the hall, he'd look right through you—walk around you like you were a stack of boxes someone had left out.

Now, Maura was everyone's favorite carp, and it was hard to imagine anyone getting on her bad side. She was unfailingly, even relentlessly cheerful, and her pigtails had led more than one newcomer to take her for a misplaced fifth-grader. No one was quite sure whether her obsession with My Little Pony was intended to be ironic or not.

But Henry managed to get on her bad side, and in a big way.

"Picking up his slack wasn't a big deal; there weren't a lot of winter projects that year. What pissed me off was knowing how much he was getting paid for taking up space."

I hadn't thought about that. Contract said that when you left the program, you were entitled to TDY pay until they returned you to the U.S. And if they couldn't get you home until November....

"This joker was earning $15 an hour, seven days a week for playing Major Tom all winter while the rest of us were busting our asses to keep the station going."

"And you didn't just chuck him and all his gear out on the Cargo berms?" Alex might be a sweetheart, but her sense of frontier justice was uncompromising.

"No, you tend to feel sorry for the guys who go toasty. At least at the start. It's sort of a 'There but for the grace of God go I' thing. And you congratulate yourself for having held it together so much better than him." She paused. "Of course, by the time September rolls around, you're just as low on T3 as he is, and duct-taping his room shut from the outside seems like a perfectly reasonable thing to do."

"You duct-taped him into his room?"

"Well, not me. I think one of the UTs did the actual job. I just signed off on the work order."

An approving smile blossomed on Alex's lips. "That's the spirit, girl."

"But hey—he was a carp. He just pulled the hinge pins and cut the tape into strips to make himself a little curtain. Left the door out in the hallway until Ben hauled it off as a fire hazard."

The change, Maura said, came in October, when they were starting to open the station up. The sun was back, sort of, slinking low around the horizon and the first flights in were only a couple of weeks away.

"So one morning Henry shows up in the galley wearing Wayfarers and a Hawaiian shirt, grinning like he's our long-lost bud and we've just rescued him from Gilligan's Island. He's all 'Dudes—we made it!' It was like he'd just woken up and thought the past six months were all a bad dream."

"And that's when…?"

"That's when we bermed him."

She gave us two beats.

"No, not really. By then we were all so toasty I don't think any of us were more pissed at him than at anyone else. By October, you've all been on the ice almost a year, and you break down into uncontrollable fits of sobbing if someone's left a tray where you normally sit. Because It's. Your. Seat. So really, there wasn't any more screaming at him than at anyone else at that point.

But Denver didn't forget. Maura liked to think the folks back at HQ had a whiteboard dedicated to Henry, covered in a grid of PostIts detailing the latest, most excruciating plans for retaliating against getting stuck with the bill for his little polar vacation.

"And the winner was?" Alex gave the countertop a drum roll.

"Well, remember: contract says they return you to U.S. soil. So I think he got dumped in Guam, after half a dozen eight-hour layovers in unpleasant places. And rumor has it that someone slipped the Loadies in Christchurch a twenty to make sure his gear ended up somewhere else.

Kathy raised her glass approvingly. "Don't fuck with the program." And we all drank.

"But," she said, "you treat them with respect, and they'll do the same for you." Her ticket home included a week in Japan, then five days in Hawaii to catch up with friends before depositing her in Anchorage for the next gig.

"And a quarter of your bonus, you bitch."

Kathy cocked her head with a victorious smile. "Don't fuck with the program." And we all drank again.

I've heard that the length of time men can drink together in silence is a function of how long they've known each other; watching Kathy swirl her glass, I wondered if the same was true for women. I knew Maura and Alex pretty well—hell, I wished I knew Alex better, but didn't every guy on station?

We let a good minute pass. Maura seemed far away, just a trace of mischief perched on the corner of her lips, while Kathy mused contently over the amber in her glass. She'd poured me a healthy shot from the bottle purporting to be Jameson's, but it didn't even taste like whiskey. No doubt someone had thought they were doing everyone a favor by consolidating a few bottles to get rid of some empties. I set the glass down and dug at my pockets, strangely unsure of what to do with my hands when I was in the Lounge and not holding a drink.

It was hard being the rookie here. Three years in, and I still had nothing that these women hadn't already heard, or seen for themselves. Sure, I had stories from back home, but there was a time and place for stories from back home, and that time was not now. For some folks here, that time was never. For some, there was no such thing as "back home" anymore, and for some, that was the way they liked it.

I'd learned, one quiet morning during a storm, that for Maura, "back home" was a 1987 Westfalia in long-term storage at the Canterbury Airpark. When she wasn't wintering over, she'd spend the New Zealand autumn as a kayak guide at Milford or Nelson, or wherever there was work. And when she was tired of that, well, you didn't have a lot of expenses down here, so there was money to let the whim carry you where it would until the ice called your name again. For a kid her age, she had a hell of a lot of stories from places that for me were just jumbled letters I couldn't even pronounce, let alone put on a map: Kalimantan, Tuvalu, Ulaanbatur.

The Ice had called all of us in different ways. You didn't just drift down to the bottom of the map and fall off the edge by accident. You jumped. You heard the call and you jumped. But I don't think any of us could explain it, any more than a moth could tell you why it's drawn to the flame.

For me, it was that cab ride back in Chicago, that storm in January when the city shut down for five days. There was an old USAP tag on his rear-view mirror. "You think this is bad?" He laughed. And once he started talking about it, he couldn't stop. He said its name in capital letters—The Ice—like you'd say the name of God, or the Devil. Like it was a living thing. He said its name like it was a woman who'd left him.

Seven years, he said. Seven years at Pole, pushing snow in an old D7 before a slipped disk one summer left him NPQ—not physically qualified. And sometimes, he said, sometimes when he first woke in the flat light of a winter morning, he still wasn't sure which was the dream, and which was his real life.

There was a bitterness behind the sadness in his eyes, but there was also a lingering wonder, an ember smoldering among the ash. It was there in the way he paused between words. Magnificent. Desolation. I couldn't tell if that was one sentence or two, but it woke some yearning in me that I'd never known I had.

He shook his head, said most folks had no idea what the hell he was talking about. But the ones that did— oh, somehow they knew.

Marie thought I was joking at first. "Well, you always did want to be an astronaut."

Her smile lasted about five seconds, just long enough for the worried silence to draw her gaze away from the southbound commuter traffic. Just long enough for her eyes to meet mine, and it was like she'd seen a ghost. I didn't have to say anything.

"Seriously? You'd really do it?"

I remember: her voice was different then. It was the voice you'd use when your doctor told you that your tests had come back and, well, there was something he needed to tell you.

I didn't know how to answer. Yes, I'd do it? Sure. If I could? The best I could manage was a nod. Yes, if I could. Seriously.

She pursed her lips—there were calculations going on a mile a minute behind that impassive, thoughtful gaze out the window.

"How long would you be gone?"

I remember that voice too. I remember the deadness and surrender in the way she said it: she said it exactly the way you'd say, "Doctor—how long do I have?"

Alex must have been watching me fidget; she pursed her lips, slid me a sympathetic, "sad puppy" frown, then lobbed a conversational log onto the fire.

"What about Flake?"

Maura shook her head—oh don't get me started. But Kathy was game. "Yeah? What about Flake?"

"Oh come on. If you want to talk about fucking with the program..."

Apparently everyone but me knew about Flake. Like I said, it takes damned near forever to hear all the stories, and it's not like anyone keeps a list.

No one could seem to remember his real name. That's the way it is on the ice: you get yourself anointed for some brilliant—or more frequently boneheaded—act of derring do, and the name your parents gave you slips away into the drifts. I could think of a dozen Polies offhand—Storm, Froggy, Dog —so firmly ingrained in my mind that it never occurred to me anyone had ever called them anything else.

"So—Flake?"

Alex said he was about five years ago. He came to Pole as a GA, a general assistant for the summer, shoveling snow and hauling crap for whoever he'd been assigned to that day.

"You'd think he'd never seen snow before. He was always, 'This is so freakin cool, man! Do you realize we're at the freakin' bottom of the freakin' world, man? The spinny part!'" Her SoCal surfer dude impression was unnerving.

So everyone pegged Flake as a prime candidate for early burnout. There was even a pool in the galley for how long he'd last. Money was on one month—two months, max. But he kept going, like the Energizer Bunny, like every day was Christmas morning. Folks would come in and say "Hey, you see the Flake Channel this morning? He was out doing snow angels in the sastrugi."

Even in January, when everyone else was slogging through the Season of Pain, Flake was Little Miss Sunshine. Started getting on people's nerves a little, but at the same time, a lot of folks sort of envied his enthusiasm.

Still, everyone was surprised when, a couple of weeks prior to redeploy, he announced that he wanted to winter over.

"A little late, wasn't it?"

"A little. Even if there'd been a position for him, we were all headed home. And to winter, he'd need to pass Psych."

"You think he would have passed?"

There was a shrug of consensus. Hell, Henry passed. And there were plenty of stories about how people gamed the psych eval. It was, as Kathy reminded us, still based on an old Navy test designed to weed out homosexuals.

Maura smirked.

"Fail?"

"Big time."

There were also perfectly innocent things that could get you knocked out of the running. "Like, when they ask how much you drink? Right answer is one or two drinks a day."

"Not zero?"

"Not zero."

"What if you don't actually drink?"

"They'll think you're lying." Alex peered at me as if

over schoolmarm glasses, then down at the putative whiskey in my hand. "And they don't like people who lie."

So yeah, she said, Flake probably could have passed Psych; he was just a little too late in the game for that year. But he started asking around, asking everybody if there was any way he could stay, asking like he'd be happy to blow Carter if it meant he didn't have to redeploy.

She let the image sink in, relishing the squeamish look on my face.

"No, I don't think he was Carter's type, but Dave's a good guy and managed to get him a late flight out, something like two days before station close. Bought him an extra week or two."

Sounded like all anyone could do, right? But then, a day before his flight, Flake disappeared.

"Yeah, gone—just like that. Carter organized a search, but we all assumed he was just hiding somewhere, hoping to miss the last flight out."

It turned out that the last person to see him had been some grad school beaker on his way to muster for redeployment. Flake had told him that the flight boomeranged, returned to MacTown with some mechanical issue. So the kid went back to his bunk to sleep off last night's going away party.

"Don't tell me."

"Ahyup. Flight came in. Flight left. On time, and with everyone on manifest aboard."

Wait—don't they check names before letting you board?

"Well yeah, but, the only guys who really care about the manifest are the loadies who come in with the plane. And they're just reading tags off parkas and matching them to what's written on their clipboard."

"So he stole the beaker's parka?"

Alex rolled her eyes at my naivety. "Didn't need to. Not all that hard to make yourself a new tag, is it? Label maker's in the supply closet. Flake probably stuck it on as he walked out to the flight line and pulled it off as soon as the Loadie had checked him in. Once he was onboard it was all one big happy, wasn't it? No one on the Herc would have any idea he wasn't supposed to be there."

I was still trying to decide whether I liked this guy. I couldn't fault his enthusiasm, but there were a lot of missing pieces.

"So he knows he can't stay at Pole. But what's he going to do at Mac Town? Wasn't he going to be flying home through Mac anyway?"

"That he was. But I guess he wanted to do it on his own terms. Maybe give himself a better chance of hiding there."

"At least better luck hiding out and surviving."

The only way you could hide at Pole was if you didn't mind them not finding your body until spring. But McMurdo, out on the edge of the Ross Sea, was damn close to being an entire town. Sure, some Polies liked to disparage it as "barely Antarctica," but it was still on the ice, and it was the logistical nerve center of the entire program; little came onto or left the continent that didn't go through Mac Town.

"Carter tried to keep it low-key, of course. He called management at Mac, but they had their hands full with other crap: that was the year the ice pier collapsed, and they were trying to get engineers in to help them figure out how to finish vessel offload before all hell really broke loose.

So they ignored it, figuring that he'd either turn up on his own, or they'd get a note from Tahiti saying, Thanks for all the fish.

It was about two weeks later that they did get a note, handwritten and slid under the NSF Rep's door at the Chalet: said Flake was holed up somewhere in town, and that he was there to stay.

Now, you can imagine how this went over, not only with Denver—they'll get hissy if someone shits without using the proper form. But Lindbeck was managing at Mac back then. He was ex-Navy, old school, and barely tolerated all the beakers running around messing up his station with their damned science experiments. There was no way he was going to tolerate some candyass pampered GA from Pole dictating terms to him. He called in the marshal and had a warrant issued for Flake's arrest. Even put up "wanted" posters in Crary, Berg and 155.

"Which, of course, was exactly the wrong thing to do. You know how folks love an outlaw. Especially in a place like Mac Town. I mean, think about it: Mac is a government base. It gets administered by federal bureaucrats half a world away, but kept running by a mix of mellow old hippies and crazy teenagers on their first time off the farm. It's a miracle the damned place actually works most of the time.

So it was pretty predictable: when Lindbeck put up those posters, he transformed Flake from some goofball into a local hero. For the hippies and the closet rebels, he was "sticking it to the man"; for everyone else, he was just good entertainment at the end of a long, hard season.

"It couldn't have been that hard to find him."

"You'd be surprised. You've got to remember that even late in the season, Mac's got what—over a thousand people? All you really need are one or two friends to keep you fed and hidden."

The marshal offered a reward and set up an anonymous tip line. But that turned into a joke right away: he'd get two or three calls a day saying Flake was on some closed-off floor in DV housing, upstairs in the fuel barn, or behind the washing machines in 211. And pretty soon it started spilling over into everything else: if there was some on-the-QT hooch party in Hotel California you didn't get invited to, you'd bust it by calling in that Flake was there. Or if you were fancying that new Strat in the music room? You'd be amazed at how much missing crap got written off as "Flake must've taken it."

Alex drifted off here for a moment, a wistful smile sneaking its way onto her face.

"But I guess Denver lost patience and decided that getting him off the Ice before station close was more important than saving face, Lindbeck's ego be damned. They found someone who could get a note to him quietly and asked what it would take to get him to turn himself in. Terms, as they liked to say, were not disclosed."

So Flake just strolled into Gallagher's one evening, looking as fresh out of the laundry as the day he arrived. And apparently there were mixed feelings when he did: some folks slapped him on the back and shook his hand for having beaten the system; others seemed more…reserved. Maybe his little escapade had screwed up their R and R. Or maybe he'd just gotten away with something they never could.

Flake told everyone he was going to spend some time on the South Island when he got off the ice. Maybe he'd head to Thailand after that; maybe he'd hike the Napali Trail. You got the idea that, whatever they settled with him, the terms didn't suck.

"But you know they'll make damned sure he'll never be back. And I'd bet a twenty that Lindbeck had his bag sent to Guam."

Kathy swirled the last of the whiskey in her glass, drained it, then set it down on the bar with an air of finality. We let the silence sink in again.

"Idiot."

"How's that, sweetie?"

"Nothing, sorry." I hadn't realized the word had come out aloud; hadn't wanted it to. But Flake had thrown it all away. Question wasn't whether you had to go—time comes, we all have to go. Question was whether you left yourself any way of getting back. I said it again, this time only in my head: Idiot.

"You think you'll ever come back?"

Kathy contemplated an answer through her empty glass and swirled it again meditatively, more through force of habit than any interest in its former contents.

"I guess it depends."

"On?"

"On a lot of things. On the money, for sure. On the timing, too. Things change fast in my line of work. Who knows where I'll be when they put the call out for next season."

She wasn't done, though—you could tell there was still something on her mind. We waited.

"Mostly I guess it depends how long it takes before I run out of stories."

A low hum rose somewhere out on the ramp. Out in the frozen everlasting sunlight, beyond the warm, dark cocoon of the Summer Camp Lounge, it grew to a whine as the Herc's engines reached takeoff power and the ponderous steel bird gathered speed. It was airborne by the time it passed us, doppler-shifting away, northbound, the only direction there was down here.

Onboard that midnight flight? Probably some old pallets of hardware getting retro'ed back to Mac Town. Packages and a batch of love letters home. Probably a few beakers, too, wide-eyed and wondrous from their two weeks Doing Science at the Bottom of the World. Clutching their precious data, yes, but holding closer to something more valuable, something they'd carry with them long after the march of science made their little ones and zeros irrelevant. Something that would be with them forever, whether or not they ever came back. Something that we, down here, tossed around like fool's gold and traded for a turn at the bottle in the Summer Camp Lounge. Go on, pour me another shot of whatever crap you're drinking. Go on, and I'll tell you another one.

Coalinga, Northbound

The thing about Gram, he was telling me, was that she always got her way. It wasn't that she was controlling or needy; it was more like she couldn't bear not being a part of everything. She'd always send the card for his birthday, usually red and frilly like a valentine. That was nice. Of course she'd call that morning to wish him a happy one, to ask about his plans for the day—that was nice, too. But the thing is, she'd have already called him the day before, to make sure he'd gotten the card ("But don't you dare open it early, Paulie!"), and the day after, to ask whether those plans had gone as he hoped. He loved her dearly, he said, but, even from four hundred miles away, she could be a bit—he paused to choose his words carefully—suffocating.

He stopped to cough and clear his throat again and assured me he wasn't contagious —isn't that what everyone says? But Paul did seem a likable guy, easygoing and quick to make friends, even in the sterile confines of the clinic. His neat but open-necked Oxford and jeans marked him as one of those thirty-something professionals who had gravitated to San Francisco not for the crazy nightlife or relentless corporate climb but for the more aesthetic pleasures that the city offered. And there was a boyish way he kept combing back the sandy blond part of an otherwise conservative haircut that he'd let—deliberately, I suspected—get just a little too long. Me? I was on my way to Bolivia next month and needed some Cipro and a few booster shots to get up to date. Him? Well, apparently we were getting to that. The long way around.

The thing was, even ignoring the risk of contagion, he was beginning to make me uncomfortable. I mean, we both had time to kill and there was no one else to talk with, but confessing your family's control issues to a total stranger didn't fall into one of the expected topics for waiting room conversation.

My unease seemed lost on Paul as he waxed nostalgic. When he was young, he said, his parents would pile him and his two sisters in the back of the family station wagon, a cavernous beige and brown Oldsmobile with fake wood trim, for the twice-yearly drive down the Central Valley to see Gram in Pasadena. The Olds had a third seat you could fold out to face backwards and look where you'd been—you know, he said, "like in the movie." But mostly they just kept it flat and threw a bunch of pillows there to give the kids a place to lie down and sleep during the hours of featureless I-5 monotony.

They had tricks to pass the time: prizes for spotting the first oil well, the first palm tree. The license plate game and working your way through the alphabet on road signs. Once in a while, down that barren four-hour stretch south of Stockton, his father would clear his throat and take a deep breath in preparation for breaking the silence. "Let's just see if there's anything on worth listening to," he'd say to no one in particular, and reach for the radio. He always started at the bottom of the FM band, turning the right-hand knob slowly, craning his neck as if listening for some faint signal from Amelia Earhart or the Lost Patrol.

Occasionally the speaker would burst into life with the sounds of Crazy Eddie's car dealership, mariachi music or the drone of a farm report; his father would listen for a half minute, gauging the station's prospects for improvement, then move on.

He never bothered with the AM—"Nothing but God and Mexicans on the AM, and I don't understand either of them," he said.

Back then, Paul said, it never occurred to him to wonder why his mother never drove. She'd always sit there to his father's right, charting their progress on the layers of AAA maps that covered the dashboard and her lap like a paper snowdrift. "Sixteen miles to Coalinga, kids," she'd announce, then do the calculations in her head. "At this rate, we'll see it in fourteen and a half minutes." Then she'd set her watch and announce, fifteen minutes later, that we were well within the margin of error and that, unless there was traffic on the Grapevine, we ought to be at Gram's by dinner.

There was, of course, no special significance to Coalinga, but there were no other towns along the way that even had highway signs until you got to Kettleman City, and she too seemed to need some way to pass the time.

Kettleman City loomed large in his memories of the trip, he said. Biggest McDonalds in the world there, or at least that's what some kid in school had told him. And it became a ritual early on that—if the kids were good—they could stop at Kettleman City and get Happy Meals ("But remember, if you fight over the toys, Mom is going to have to take them all away"). They never fought much anyway, and even if they did, his father always found some excuse to forgive them; Paul figured his father needed the break more than they did, and sat outside in the shade of the Hamburglar and Mayor McCheese-themed umbrellas taking long slow draws on one of the Marlboros he kept stashed in the glove box.

They'd always make it to Pasadena on time, or within his mother's "margin of error" and settle into the clockwork ritual of Dinner at Gram's. The house sat up at the base of the mountain, small, neat and white, like some miniaturized colonial outpost misplaced in the hills of Southern California. She met them at the door, invariably aproned with oven mitt in hand, as though to emphasize that she'd spent the day preparing for them and was just stepping away from the kitchen for the first time, to offer them welcome. She'd line them up as soon as they were inside: "Now Theresa, you're sure you're not stealing Paulie's dinner under the table? You'll be twice as tall as him, the way you're growing. And Mary—oh, look how lovely you are!" Mary wasn't, not particularly, and it didn't bother her, but as much as Gram's observations tended toward the wishful, the children had been warned not to contradict her. "It gives her pleasure," their mother said, "So please—please, please just smile and say 'I'm glad you think so.'"

The Naugahyde waiting room chair creaked as Paul leaned back, cleared his throat again and looked up wistfully. "That may be the most important sentence anyone ever taught me," he said. "I'm glad you think so."

Dinner itself was always spaghetti and meatballs. Always. Gram presided from the head of the table, ladling her blended-smooth tomato sauce over everything from a gold-edged china tureen, but when Paul asked for extra meatballs, he liked to keep them separate, on the side, to sprinkle salt on and eat dry, bite by bite at the end of his fork.

Then, once the plates were cleared, it was time for The Piano. He couldn't remember a time when he didn't think of it being spelled that way—an entity, an ordeal singular and significant enough to warrant being capitalized out of awe and fear: The Bomb, The Plague. The Piano.

Naturally, all three kids had been expected to learn to play. Ostensibly by their father, who contended that skill with a musical instrument was one of the basic hallmarks of a well-bred member of society. But his formulaic repetition of the pronouncement betrayed it as something that had been imposed upon him as a child, and they dared not risk the consequences of asking what it implied for their own mother, who played nothing.

So Theresa, Mary, and Paul endured weekly lessons with Mrs. Weiner on Channing Avenue, promising to practice for 30 minutes every evening except Sundays. Mary took to the challenge earnestly in the spirit of a middle child, tackling Chopin and Liszt with enthusiasm. Theresa, always the rebel, plonked and banged the keyboard in a manner that seemed to be calculated to madden Mrs. Weiner, and was eventually given permission to switch to guitar, which she taught herself with the help of cassette tapes from the local library.

It was Paul, the youngest, who always struggled, putting in—sure, not 30 minutes every day, but enough that he should have been making progress. And progress, in this family, meant having something new to play for Gram on each of those twice-yearly pilgrimages south.

At Gram's, Theresa would always have her out: she "forgot" to pack the guitar twice before her father insisted on seeing it in the car prior to leaving the house. And even then, she managed to forestall a lengthy recital by launching into her rendition of something by Black Flag, the Sex Pistols or Circle Jerks. Eventually, she was simply excused from the entire exercise.

By that point Mary had mastered not only the keyboard itself but all of the graces that surrounded Gram's idea of a recital. She would face her mostly reluctant audience with the sheet music held between pinched fingers and intone the title of the piece to be played in the manner of an English butler, then bow slightly and seat herself, poised above the keyboard for just a breath before launching into some dizzying Bach invention.

Her performance further accentuated the contrast with Paul's lack of skill, even on the so-called "beginner's pieces." On a good day he might make it a half dozen bars in before stumbling, retrying a phrase a few times, and restarting the whole thing from the beginning. By the third attempt, Gram was praising his perseverance and asking if anyone else would like more coffee.

"You know, Paulie," she'd say later in the evening, "Skill is good, but stick-to-it-iveness is better. As long as you're practicing. You are practicing, aren't you?"

He was, and said so, and she believed him. It will come, she promised. It will come.

Paul sat back here, checked his watch and looked up at the clock above the table of neatly-arranged *Family Circle* and *Sunset* magazines. He made some offhand comment about doctors and why they're called "waiting rooms," coughed once into a handkerchief, then leaned in to continue.

It was about a month ago that he got the call from his mother. Gram had been in decline for quite a while, but seemed to be hanging on without too much discomfort. The birthday phone calls had stopped long ago and the cards, when they still came, were now written in an unfamiliar hand—Paul assumed that of the hospice nurse—with only the brief scrawl of her once-elegant signature at the bottom. When they did speak (now it was Paul who called on her birthdays), she would ask how his piano lessons were progressing and he had learned to lie convincingly—he saw no point in denying her such a small pleasure.

Then it was his mother on the phone, saying how Gram had gone peacefully—Paul raised his hands slightly from the arms of his chair when he said "peacefully," as if to suggest that I extrapolate an implied set of air-quotes. And his mother said that, seeing as how Gram wished to be cremated, there would be no funeral per se. But she was flying down to help with the estate and expected that they'd have some sort of memorial service he'd need to come to Pasadena for.

The old house looked remarkably unchanged. College, then study abroad, then his marriage to Mark had pulled him farther afield over the years, providing increasingly plausible reasons for missing those family reunions. By the time he and Mark returned to the Bay Area, the spell of the ritual had been broken—how long had it been since he'd seen her in person? But the cheerful-if-dated silver and red candy stripe wallpaper still hung in the dining room. The low coffee table by the fireplace was still arrayed with those small cut crystal bowls of cashews and pistachios, so vivid in his memory that he wondered whether they'd all simply remained there, untouched since his childhood. Mary flew in early from Boston and Theresa drove down from Sedona, looking surprisingly subdued and respectful. And there was mom and Aunt Ginny and all the uncles whose names he could never remember, but who didn't seem to mind, and everyone was milling around more like it was a cocktail party than a memorial service.

There were speeches and toasts, the common theme of which seemed to be that Gram had had a good life, and had lived it exactly the way she wanted. The older folks seemed to chuckle a little whenever this last point was made. When it was all over and he and Mary were cleaning up the last of the paper plates, his mother came to him with a look of sympathy.

"So, Paulie, I know you weren't all that close to her, but she always admired you. 'He's got that stick-to-itiveness,' she'd always say, once you were out of earshot."

He thanked her, but she had more to tell him.

"The thing is, we were going through the will, and…"—now she had his complete attention, and he turned to face her. His mother drew a full breath. "She wants you to have the piano."

He was caught off guard by his own laugh.

"Yes, I know. I know it doesn't fit into your life, and I'm pretty sure it doesn't fit into your apartment. But it clearly gave her pleasure to know that it was going to you. You and your stick-to-it-iveness."

Now, she laughed too, in the same voice. Of course she knew about his polite fictions and appreciated the irony of the gift as much as anyone. But then she was serious again.

"Would you at least keep it for a little while?"

He promised he would, and reserved a Ryder truck for the following weekend.

He and Mark would drive down on Saturday morning, load the piano up with help from the kids at Starving Students Movers, and drive back the next morning. The folks at DC Musical had introduced him to someone local who claimed they could get it through his front door and into the living room when they got home, and they figured that they'd take it from there when the time came. Maybe they'd keep the piano after all. Maybe he would try learning again, and maybe this time it would all click.

Honestly, he said, the piano itself wasn't anything special: a 1922 Gulbransen Baby Grand in walnut. Maybe if it were expertly restored, but Gram's looked like it had been refinished by a weekend hobbyist in hardware store varnish, with smears and drips frozen in time. Somewhere, Paul remembered from his childhood, there had even been the remains of a fly caught as if in amber. No, it wasn't an heirloom by any stretch of the imagination, but it was Gram's and he had to take it.

His mother called again on Friday night, asking one more favor.

"You can't imagine how awkward I feel asking you to do this," she said. It was just that Gram's urn—well, they wouldn't mail it, and seeing as how Paul was going to be in Pasadena anyway...

Sure, he said. He'd bring the urn back too.

The tire blew out two miles short of Coalinga, northbound in the passing lane. Paul was driving, using Gram's brass urn as an armrest while Mark leaned over from the right seat, trying to get his Sam Shepard audiobook to play on the stereo. The steering buckled, and the truck left the highway sideways, flipping as it careened off the drainage ditch and tearing through nearly a hundred yards of roadside scrub before coming to rest on its side.

Highway Patrol said that, all things considered, they were very lucky. Airbags on those big trucks didn't often work they way they were supposed to, and the lack of a front impact meant that the energy of the crash was dissipated slowly. Paul pulled the collar of his shirt of his shirt sideways, revealing a dark bruise running down from his shoulder where the seatbelt had caught him, then thought better of it. "Sorry—I'm oversharing, aren't I?" No, no, it was okay.

Mark had fared a little worse: a concussion on the right from where his head hit the side window, and lacerations on the left from Gram's tumbling urn. Turns out those things can be dangerous, he said. But they were both fine, really.

And the piano? It had parted ways with the truck when they hit the drainage ditch. The family in the Chevy Impala a few lengths back said it went straight up, as if launched by a giant catapult when the truck disappeared in a tumbling cloud of desert dust. "It was turning over, like in slow motion, like it was flying away," the wife said, "I knew I should be looking after whoever was in that poor truck and praying for them, but I couldn't take my eyes off that piano."

When it did come to earth, the Gulbransen left a trail of debris they never did find the end of. Paul had driven back the following week, mostly out of curiosity, and spent half the afternoon tracing the trail of impacts. Every time he thought he'd found the end of it, there'd be a glint of light further on, a brass fitting or ivory key thrown just a little farther. He gathered a handful of them—he didn't know why—and left the rest for the insurance company to deal with.

He sat back now and shrugged his shoulders like there was nothing left to say, then erupted in another fit of coughing, which he tried to smother with the handkerchief that had never left his hand.

"Oh, right, right," he said, once he'd recovered his breath. "Gram."

"Gram?" The way he said it, it seemed he thought invoking her name explained something.

"Yeah, Gram."

It took a couple of minutes for Paul and Mark to come to their senses and kick open the driver's side door of the destroyed truck, and they climbed out with the assistance of the husband in the Impala. Mark was bleeding and disoriented and both were coughing heavily, but by the time the Highway Patrol arrived, it was clear that neither was seriously injured. Still, it took a while to make sense of the fine gray dust that covered them both from head to toe.

He looked me dead in the eye with a wry smile and waited.

"Gram?"

"Gram."

Yeah, he said, he lost the piano, but they still have the urn. And he likes to think she'd be happy to know that he'll always carry a bit of her—he coughed again, deliberately this time, and thumped his chest—right here inside of him.

Everybody Has a Plan

"Why don't we ever go to the Cubberleys' house any more for dinner?"

Like most of Olivia's questions from the back seat of the family's aging Honda, it seemed to tumble from the sky like a maple leaf. Perhaps it *was* a maple leaf, her mother thought; the light caught them just so on the roadside line of trees, and perhaps it reminded her of maple syrup, which reminded her of Sunday mornings when the family all ate together, slowly, while Jack presided over the grill, serving up custom creations on demand with mock pomp. "Make me one shaped like a dinosaur, Daddy!" she'd say. And he would.

This would remind her of how, with syrup-sticky plates still covering the table, they would talk about the day ahead, how there was still time before everyone had to get dressed—time for comics and Nintendo—just a little, before they needed to get ready for the drive up to the city to see Gramma Jane and Grampa Alan. How Grampa Alan had an old phonograph, with stacks of wax cylinders that would make scratchy sounds of singers from long, long ago if you could just figure out how to make it work right. And how they'd gotten it to work, once, but now Grampa Alan said he thought something was broken in the springs, so it sat on the shelf, just above where Olivia could see without standing on her tiptoes. That, she thought, would make her think of Henry's—Mr.

Cubberley's—workshop and how, when she followed him down the stairs after dinner, he would point out all the different projects he was working on, and how she was sure he could fix anything on earth.

"Why do you ask, honey?"

"Just wondering."

There was room now, room in the pause afforded by the Honda's bouncing progress, room in the distance between her, peering through the afternoon light for a hidden street sign on the tree-covered lane, and Olivia, musing in back seat. Room not to try and answer that question right now.

Henry always seemed like such a perfect father, didn't he? Jack probably did as well. Perhaps they all did until you knew them better. So who was it that thought of her as the perfect mother, the perfect wife? Anyone?

But Henry—oh, how he would sit with the kids, explaining how the magnet worked while he showed them, patiently, how to wrap the wire around and around, lining up each turn around the big steel bolt as neatly as…oh, as something. She couldn't really think what. Then he'd hook the battery up and they'd explore the workshop, Olivia and the Cubberley boys together, picking up old nails and loose washers with the magnet, carrying them to table at arm's length and —with a flick of the wire—letting them drop into paper cups he'd set out for them.

And how he'd always be the first on his feet after dinner, when it was time to clear the dishes. Sheila would make a half-hearted attempt to help, but he'd stop her: "I'll get them, honey; you sit and keep the Masons company." Maybe he was just being sweet;

maybe he was restless. Or maybe there was something there in the room, something too subtle for her to detect, and he needed fresh air.

She hated that she never seemed to pick up on these things. Wasn't that what women's intuition was supposed to be about? Jack always teased her about it —gently, of course. "What? I thought that was part of the package; didn't we have it in the prenup? Section Five, Paragraph Two, right? Wife certifies that she's equipped with fully-functioning woman's intuition."

On better days, she'd tease him right back.

She heard Olivia shift, restlessly, in her seat. "You need something, Oli? Are you hungry?"

"Can I have chips?"

There it was, she thought, with a touch of satisfaction. But only for the children. She could never ever tell what Jack was thinking, even when he said he had tried to tell her. If she sat across the table and watched him carefully, focused, sometimes she could make out the words he wanted to say: I'm tired, I need more space, more affection, more…something. But it was only sometimes—like she was trying to read his lips after the words themselves were lost in the storm that engulfed them both.

"Mommy?"

Oh, right: chips. "I've got Pringles in my bag. You can eat them while I'm in my meeting."

The thing was, it wasn't Jack's storm; he was always the rock—fixed and impassive among the wind and crashing waves. If life were a Monopoly game, Jack's piece would be a little mountain, the Rock of Gibraltar. No, the storm was hers, and hers alone; she pictured her own Monopoly piece: a tiny tornado cast out of blue plastic, or whatever they made Monopoly pieces out of these days. Everything seemed so complicated for her, so fraught with implications, entanglements and consequences swirling around her head. It always came out of nowhere: a simple request—brownies for the school play, for example—that rippled into questions about nut allergies, and who needed to be asked and how to reach them, and the other calls she needed to make but didn't have time because she had to go shopping and... she only realized how loud her voice had become when she saw the frightened look in Olivia's eyes. After days like those, Jack would find her curled into the couch around some thick book with dragons and princesses on the cover, the remains of a bowl of popcorn littering the floor at her feet.

"I know how you feel, honey," he once told her, crouching beside where she lay. "I feel that way too, sometimes. Really." A pause as he squeezed her hand. "And you know, when I do, I've been trying to follow Sheila's advice. She says that there's some sort of 'energy turbine'—that's what she calls it, an energy turbine. She says she forces herself to put energy in by going to the gym or something, and it comes out as more energy that lets her do the stuff she needs to do."

"Just shut up about Sheila, would you?" The anger in her words surprised her.

"Look, I'm sorry. I'm trying to help. I'm trying to fix things. That's what I do, isn't it?"

She looked up, studying him from her nest of pillows: earnest, hurt, frustrated. Yes, he was trying to fix things, the poor dear. But couldn't he understand that sometimes, just sometimes, she didn't want things to be fixed? That sometimes all she wanted was that word of sympathy, of commiseration, that word of assurance that he loved her, just as she was.

How did Sheila manage? She had three kids (three!) and still managed to look—okay, she'd say it—fabulous. Five days at the gym every week, boxing lessons, volunteering at the Children's Museum, oil painting, writing and still being a perfect mother to those boys. And beautiful, smart, kind—you wanted to hate her, but couldn't.

A storm—a different storm—rose in her, and she clawed her way to the safety of the task at hand: 7515 Loyola Way; he'd said there would be a sign, and the street numbers were going in the right direction. Couldn't be more than a few blocks.

"How do you do it?" She'd asked one morning over coffee.

"It's the gym. I'd die if I weren't always on my way to the gym."

"I've tried the gym, Sheila. I've spent weeks going nowhere on those damned bicycles. Just makes me more tired, sitting there, spinning, thinking about all the other stuff I should be doing right now."

"The bikes? Oh god, I know what you mean: the bikes are useless."

"So what do you do at the gym?"

"Depends on what I need."

A moment of silence; thoughts running in too many directions at once.

"And what sorts of things do you need?"

She wished she could remember Sheila's face when she'd asked the question; was there anything? A trace of recognition? But she hadn't known yet, not really, and hadn't been looking; there'd been a sound from

Olivia upstairs, or from the kitchen. Or maybe her mind had just run off of its own accord, and she was wondering whether she should get more coffee, or freshen up the tray of biscuits and...

"That depends on what the morning's been like. If I was able to get the boys to school and Henry out of the house with matching socks then I usually just go for basic weight training. I don't understand how it works, but just hauling around on some dead weights gets me as buzzed as a Starbucks Mocha Frappuccino Heart Attack."

"And with less than half the calories!" She'd cocked her head, trying to sound like a TV announcer touting the latest fad, but now it sounded stupid to her, and she hated herself for saying it.

Sheila was unruffled. "Yeah, but before anything else, I always start with a run. Fifteen minutes on a treadmill, or out on the track if I've got stuff to work through."

"Stuff?" A momentary panic—should she be taking notes?

"You know—mom stuff. When the kids have just used my new Tory Burch as a cape, or when Henry says, 'Hey honey, I know we were planning on a quiet night, but I've invited the team over, and....' I know he means well, but when he does that I've got two choices: I can tear his head off, or I can get out on the track and run like hell."

"Isn't that what the boxing is for?"

"Oh, no, no, sweetheart. You don't want to go punching your way out of that sort of feeling."

"So what is the boxing for?"

"Clarity."

"Clarity?"

"Clarity."

There was another silence and she wondered if it was her turn to talk again. But Sheila had only paused for dramatic effect, gathering her words.

"All of this stuff—running, weights, biking, if that's your thing—it's you acting on the world. You're in complete control, and there's nothing coming back, nothing to help you get centered. You've got your shopping list going, and that latest stupid song you're sick of, and whether the carpet cleaner is going to be able to get dog barf out of the rug. You go running with all that in your head? It'll help you turn the volume down, but it's all still there. Weights? Same.

"But that's the thing about boxing—I swear, it was a revelation to me. I mean, it was fun spending time on the bag, spending time on posture and footwork. It's like aerobics, you know. But it was that first time in the ring, dancing around there with my coach, throwing punches at him and he said 'Okay, now I'm going to take a swing at you,' and he did. And I ducked it, because he was taking it easy on me, and he threw a few more my way. And I was getting into a rhythm, and really liking it. Even had a little sound track going in my head, like I was Rocky or something.

"Then… BAM!"

"What!?"

"He didn't hit me hard. I mean, it was just a tap by boxing standards, and what with the gloves and head guard, I don't suppose it even hurt. But Jesus Christ, he punched me right in the face, just like that. So fast I didn't even see him pull back, let alone see it coming. And everything just fell away. It was like he'd flipped a switch, and all of the noise in the world suddenly stopped. And all that crap in my head about global warming and Crimea and shopping and carpets and Henry and the kids? It was gone, and there was just me standing there flat-footed in the ring with Rudy. And it was like I was able to hear and see and think clearly for the first time in my life.

"He hit you?"

"It's what he said he was going to do, right? It's what I was paying him for."

"Yeah, but…"

"Anyhow, I think I scared him for a second—I guess I was just standing there, straight as a board, like my brain had gone off. He stopped and said something like, 'You okay?' and I said 'Yeah.' And he asked if I'd ever been hit before, and I shook my head no. And he asked if I wanted to take a break, and I told him 'Hell no.' Then he got an odd kind of a smile and said that sometimes that happens the first time you get hit. And he says I got back into my tuck with a crazy look on my face and put my guard up and said, 'Try that again.' He still teases me about it: 'Try that again.'" She said that last bit in a husky, Latino accent, bobbing her head like a prizefighter.

"So you liked it."

Sheila looked at her sideways, like she wasn't sure if she was being teased. "No, not like that." Then she settled back and gazed up at the ceiling. "But yeah. It was…useful."

"You mean in case you need to punch somebody out for stealing your perfect hubby?"

There it was, just like that. The saucer under Sheila's cup missed the edge of the coffee table and hit the floor sideways with a decisive crack and the sound of scattering porcelain.

She was out of her seat, scooping the slivers into her palm, protesting over Sheila's stammered apologies, saying that it was nothing, that these were cheap Pottery Barn cups and that they had a dozen more of them in the cupboard. When she looked up, she saw that Sheila had gone pale.

That was the last time they'd spoken.

"Okay Oli, hop on out. We're here."

The trees had given way to a block that looked like a small, forgotten neighborhood from another time and place: a long-closed service station on the corner punctuating low industrial cinderblock warehouses. The address was here, third building from the end, its incongruous sign looking oddly professional against the season-scarred walls. She pulled into a spot in the half-empty lot and let the engine die, catching herself spinning half a dozen excuses for starting the car again, for just driving away. She didn't have time for this. This wasn't what people like her did. She didn't belong here. But…wasn't it trying to belong that had brought her to this point?

She held the girl's hand as they pushed open the tinted glass door and raised her voice to be heard over the unexpected din. "I don't know how this is going to go, Oli, but when I talked with Mr. Ramirez, he said there was a quiet place you could sit and read. I've got your chips and juice box here, and we'll get you settled before we begin."

The woman hunched behind the metal desk looked up expectantly. Broad shouldered and wide hipped, with beautifully-defined muscles tracing the contours of her arms; she could have been an art student's anatomical study, if not for the sweaty tank top and gym shorts. Behind her, rough percussive sounds echoed unevenly over the concrete floor.

"Heya. Can I help you?"

"Yes—I'm here to see Rudy Ramirez."

"And this is about...?"

"Boxing lessons. I need to learn how to take a punch."

On Ziahtown Road

The old man had come to the side of the road to die. His daughter had gone to Ziahtown a week ago, on market day. Sometimes she stayed with her mother's people there overnight, sometimes longer. He didn't mind—he was fine on his own in the village, and he knew women needed others to talk to. But when she didn't return on the third day, he walked the narrow dirt footpath through the forest, following the river to the main road. There he sat and asked passersby whether they were going to Ziah, and if they would ask after his daughter when they got there. The next morning he came again to the road and sat. Again he asked his questions, but no one had seen her.

The old man had gone to Ziahtown himself, many times, when he was younger. Back then, he had gone to drink palm wine with other young men, to brag, and to court his wife. Now? Now Ziah was too far, much too far for an old man to walk. Even the walk from his village to the road was hard for him. He had started early, as soon as it was warm enough. But without his daughter to make the fire and cook porridge, it had been hard to shake off the night's chill. There was still a little dried fish and fruit—the last of the boiled rice had gone bad two days before—so he ate some of the fish to fill his belly and warm himself; he placed the rest, with the fruit, in his shoulder bag and started toward the road.

There used to be more families here in Gbagee—his brother's family, and before the war even more than that. When Taylor's men came, they took the boys, and yes, many of the girls too, and the rest fled. His brother had always been the clever one—when they'd heard Taylor was coming, he'd burnt his own home and hid his family in the bush for a week. He hid by the bamboo on the other side of the river, where there was water and noise, and it was hard to travel. The brother had told them all what to do, and told them what Taylor would do when he came. But Gbagee was so small—why would a big man like Charles Taylor bother Gbagee?

Yes, his brother had always been the clever one, the old man thought. His boys had hidden, then come back to Gbagee to grow tall and strong at their father's side. His own? They were gone. His girls—they had been taken by Taylor's men, too. They left only his youngest, just walking then and weaned by his brother's wife—he called the little girl Jewel, his own wife's last gift.

Things were better after the war, and then men from the mines came through. They said there was gold in Konobo, and the Chinese were paying workers to dig for it. One of the men who came was from Jeway, and the old man's brother knew him, and sent a son to go with him to see. The son sent back money, so when the rains ended, his brother's family left too.

His oldest daughter returned—she had been taken by Taylor's men, but she came back after the war. She had with her a small boy she called James. The reunion had been happy and the boy thrived. The old man carried him on his shoulders, and taught him songs.

He showed the boy how to plant cassava, how to tap the rubber trees. Then the daughter fell ill and weakened. She grew thin and wouldn't eat. James sat at the foot of her bed while Jewel sponged her sister's forehead with a wet cloth. The bush doctor from Geleglor told her to take peppers, to breathe the smoke from the leaves he brought, but it did not help, and she died early in the next rainy season. James fell ill soon after, and by the time the rains stopped, only the old man and Jewel were left.

Even before, Gbagee had never been a large village, not like Bilibo City or Ziah, but why should it be? They had enough. If you wanted oil or cloth, the women could walk to Ziah and be back by nightfall. Even faster if someone on the trail with a motorbike gave you a ride. And Bilibo? The old man couldn't think why anyone would go to Bilibo. The Germans had come and built three wells in Bilibo. He walked there himself three years ago and asked them to build one—just one—in Gbagee. It took the whole morning to get to Bilibo, and he wasn't a young man, not even back then. He had dressed well to meet the Germans, and he spoke well to them. He told them the history of Gbagee—how they fought well in the war, and how they thrived and now fell on hard times. Of how many goats he had and how much better it would be to have a well for his daughter to draw from. The Germans listened and thanked him for his speech. But they said the choice was not theirs, that they had been sent by others who decided to build the wells here. Could he talk to those others? It was very difficult, they said. The old man thought how for the foreigners, simple things always seemed so difficult.

The sun was still low when he made it to the road this morning, and he was now grateful for the coolness of the still air. When he was younger, he had never even noticed the time it took to come this far, only the first step of a journey, but now he was tired, and happy to be done walking. He had needed to stop many times along the way, to set down his cane and recline against a fallen tree, to prop up his bad leg and soothe the swollen knee with his hands. When he did, he could hear monkeys playing, fighting by the river.

It was good that the monkeys had come back. After the war, the forest was silent—not even the birds sang. There was not much meat on a drongo or pitta, but there was not much meat anywhere—the boys wove fish nets from the reeds and caught what they could. Now, he told himself, things were good, and the forest was full of life. Only Gbagee was empty.

"Eku ale, Dada!"

The woman hailed him in Krahn as she came down the rise. He knew her as a cousin of his wife's family. He called back to her, welcoming her, and waited for her to approach, two girls in tow and a boy on her back.

"What are you doing alone on the road this morning, Abraham? Are you going to Bilibo?"

He told her he had no use for Bilibo. Then where? Nowhere, child. He had come to the road so he would not die alone. So his body would not be found by animals.

She chided him, again using his Christian name, and silenced her children. You cannot be joking about death like that, grandfather, she said. You know the devil comes when he is called.

He looked up at her from where he sat—she was a strong woman, like his wife had been. Her sash and skirt were clean and bright, beautiful blue, reds and gold wrapped across her tall and sturdy frame. Her cheeks were full and round, and her brow glistened with the trace of sweat that told of the miles she'd already walked this morning. The children too, he saw —fine girls, they were, tall like their mother. They each balanced a broad woven bowl of palm nuts on their head, and the older one was now resting on a large plastic oil can she had been carrying in her right hand. They were dressed richly, those two, and the boy was fat and healthy.

You are doing well, daughter, he told the woman, and praised the health of her children. Your father's family grows strong and large. How is your uncle? Is Uncle Garley with us still? His wife? He didn't listen to her answer, though—Garley was a fine man who had welcomed him in his time and given a generous dowry with his daughter. But now he simply wanted to turn the woman's attention away from where he sat. She was still too young to understand such things.

When she stopped talking, he let the sound of the forest fill in for conversation. The monkeys were still fighting, though farther off, and the sharp, bright call of finches spun overhead like a hundred rusty wheels. He nodded toward the road—You have far to go, he said, and the morning is already warm. You should not waste your time on an old man. The woman looked at him, her face now sober. I will ask again after your Jewel, she said. Maybe she had to go to Zwedru—but I am sure she will return soon.

When he was alone again, he reached into his pocket for tobacco and was suddenly embarrassed for how he must have appeared to the woman. His pants were shabby and fringed in mud and sap from the walk. His shirt, the orange and black one Jewel had brought him from Ziah during the festival, was torn where he had fallen—was that two days ago?—and there was dirt and blood around the tear. The fall had not bothered him; he was used to pain. But he was now sad at having torn the shirt, and for how pitiful he must have looked to the woman.

The old man did not want pity. He leaned forward to retrieve his cane and hoisted himself upright, mindful to spare the weight on his tender knee, but still wincing from the pain of the effort. There was a place on the river, not far back along the path, where he could wash himself. Yes, he should have thought of this before: if one is to die with any dignity at all, one needs to be clean.

He found the place where the shallow bank was lined with broad flat rocks that dipped under the water. He and his brother played there many times when they were young. If you stripped back the spine of a palm frond, you could tie it into a snare and fish here for small eels between the rocks. The old man had been very good at this—he could wait patiently, motionless with his snare placed in the water just so. And it seemed he always knew where the eel was hiding, and precisely where it would next poke its head out. The brother had no such patience, and twirled his stick to make patterns that rippled and spread in the water.

You will never catch anything like that, the boy—
not yet an old man—said. But his brother was bored
with the game of waiting and splashed his stick
deeper, now swinging it to slice the end into the water
and spray the boy. He lost his temper that time, the old
man remembered, and their mother scolded them both
for the torn clothes.

More often, their games were woven into the work
they had to do, and they played well together, like the
brothers they were. When it was time to clear the
fields, they were giants, uprooting villages of
underbrush with their bare hands or warriors, dealing
death to the enemy bamboo with broad swings of their
father's machete. At harvest time they were gold
miners and treasure hunters, unearthing the hidden
riches of the cassava underground.

Children from the other families—Virgil and Marcus
and the others—would lure them into forest games,
playing at the hunt when chores were done. One of
them was the wild boar hiding in the underbrush to
catch the unwary hunters who sought it. Or they
would climb trees and call to each other like monkeys,
each trying to hang from the branches in the most
ludicrous way they could think of. The old man
marveled that none of them ever actually fell.

And when their mother made them go to the
schoolhouse, they would always find ways to make
games of their studies there. Mrs. Felicity didn't seem
to mind, as long as they finished their work.

Evenings they told stories, some they had learned
from their parents, and some they just made up to pass
the time. Stories of when the animals could talk, and
how great great grandfather had made a bargain with

Lion. Back then, Lion had a smooth black coat like his cousin the Jaguar, and he was the best hunter in the forest. But he could not resist the smell of meat cooking in the village and was always getting in trouble with the villagers. One day when he came to the village, great great grandfather pleaded with him—you are such a great hunter and we are so poor, he said. If you teach us how to hunt, we will teach you how to make fire and cook meat. So Lion taught the men of the village how to hunt—how to sneak up on their prey and surprise it with sharp knives. In exchange, they showed him how to make fire and roast meat on long poles. But Lion was both lazy and impatient, and one day he grew tired of waiting for his meat to cook over the fire. He said to himself "If I eat the fire, then all the meat I eat will cook inside me." But when he did, his hair all stood on end and turned the color of flame.

This was the old man's favorite story, and when he told it, he tucked his chin in and made a booming voice for the lion, just the way his uncle had done when he was scaring the rest of the the village boys. Of course the boys knew that the stories weren't true, but they still loved to hear them.

The old man tucked his chin and made the booming voice now, just for himself, and looked in the water for his reflection. There was a stranger there with a wrinkled face full of white stubble and lost, crazy eyes. No, but of course—the realization came over him as his reverie faded. He had not shaven since the day after Jewel left for Ziah. Yes, he could do it himself, but it was a clumsy task, and she was so adept with his old razor—he figured he would wait until the next day, when she came back, and let the beard grow a little.

Back at the road, he set himself again on the low wooden platform and waited. He was no longer waiting for his daughter, and no longer waiting for other passersby to bring him news. He was waiting for what he thought must just happen when there was nothing left to do.

The platform was a simple one, three flat-split planks bound together with wire, raised to sitting height above the ground on a pair of short logs laid at each end. If the old man lay lengthwise, it could serve as a bed, and not an uncomfortable one at that. Or a bier. No, he would not lie down now, not yet. He ran his hand along the worn front edge of the platform— his brother had built this one, as he had built everything wooden that still stood in Gbagee. He was a good man, this brother, the old man thought, and felt no spite at his leaving.

When the birds fell silent, the old man closed his eyes to listen—yes, there was a motorbike coming. There were more of them now than in the past, but the road here was still difficult for them—when he last walked to Gao, he passed three young men in the river below, trying to retrieve the wreckage of a motorbike that had slipped from the smooth round log the village used as a bridge. A man could get hurt on one of those, he thought then.

The sound grew louder, and he could now tell that it was coming from the west, from direction that led to Ziahtown. He straightened his back, sitting upright now, and rested his hands in his lap. He wanted whoever passed to see him with the dignity of his age, not as a ragged old man who was waiting to die. But wasn't he? Never mind—an old man could wait to die with dignity as well.

The motorbike crested the hill and descended toward him, its engine clattering at a rough idle. He did not know these boys, the large one driving, or the two who clung on behind. The driver waved and called a greeting when they passed, a polite greeting, but he did not slow, and the engine whined in protest, spitting blue smoke as they began to climb the path away from him, toward Bilibo.

A tanager called tentatively as the sound of the motorbike faded over the hill. It was joined by others, then the finches resumed their rusty wheel chorus and the forest was again as it had been. The sun was warm now, and he could feel the last traces of damp leave the folds of his river-washed shirt and trousers. How natural the sun felt, he thought, and wondered if he'd miss it, wondered if he'd feel anything once life had left him.

He'd never been one to spend too much time worrying about an afterlife—there was always too much to do here and now, to gather cassava and clear land. The pang of worry struck him suddenly: what if this was why Gbagee had not thrived? Yes, he and his family had tended the burial ground and made their offerings during the seasons. He had observed the proper rites for his daughter and for James. These he had done it out of grief, but the rest? It was done out of habit, deference to custom. Maybe the ancestors really were watching, maybe they did care, and were chastising him for his indifference. Well, the old man thought, there was no point in worrying now—he would find out soon enough.

For now the sun was warm, and that gave him comfort. He hoped that death would find him during the day, while it was still warm like this—night had always troubled him, and he did not want to pass another one alone.

He had woken many times in the night, looking out at the dark sky, its hem torn by the jagged line of silhouetted trees ringing the house. Each time he let his eyes and mind adjust to the idea of being awake, he thought of how each hour of the night had its own fear, its own demon. The one just passed had filled itself with shapeless terrors, monsters grown giant from the seeds of yesterday's cares. The next hour, as the eastern sky showed its first tinges of the morning's promise would bring sadness, resignation. But there, in the moment, he felt only loathing, a loathing for himself and how he had allowed his village to wither. When he died, it would be gone entirely, and there would be no one to tend the graves, or—in a few years—even remember where they were.

He became aware again of the warmth of the sun on his face, and this brought him back to the day, here, by the side of the road to Ziahtown. The sadness was gone—he had done what he could, and it was not enough.

The old man thought back to the missionaries who had come to Gbagee. It was not long after James died, and the two men said they had come to provide comfort, and to spread the Gospel. The older one was dressed in crisp black and white, and spoke while the younger man, barely older than his Jewel, stood behind, nodding and smiling. They explained that because the boy had died before the Gospel came to him, he would spent a while in limbo before being led to paradise. But the old man could go to paradise and see his child as soon as he died, if he would only accept Jesus as his savior.

And if he didn't? If he continued in the way he always had? He'd heard the missionaries talk before, and their stories sounded even more improbable than those of the Gio elders. The missionaries looked at him gravely—if he turned away from the word of Jesus he would face eternal damnation in a fiery hell. The old man thought about this for a minute before asking his next question, and he asked it slowly. Tell me, he said, if had I died before you brought me this Gospel, would I also have gone to limbo, then to paradise? Yes, they said—that is what we believe. The old man raised his chin in the manner of the village chiefs he remembered and waited until the missionaries met his eyes again— he wanted to make sure they were paying attention. You are telling me that if you had not come I would go to paradise. And now with your teaching, with this "gift" you bring, I am likely to go to hell? He chased them from the village with his cane.

The heat of the sun, now overhead, told him it was time to eat. If he were in the field with cassava, this would be when he and James took to the cool broad shadows of the banana palm. They would sit, and as he broke off pieces of the cornmeal cake, he would tell the boy a story, and James would draw pictures in the dirt with a sharp stick to go along. Is that the monkey, James? No, Grandpa, no—don't you see? It's the motorbike Ikumi is riding. Here are the wheels. But now I'll draw the monkey for you—here, see? And he would nod—yes, yes, of course. How clever the boy was, and how eager to please, even when he was wracked with fever, and his limbs were swollen from the sickness. It is all right, Grandpa, he would say. I am still drawing, only now the pictures are just in my head —can you still see them?

The old man opened his bag and looked at what remained of the fish and fruit—no, he wasn't hungry —but it was the time to eat. That, at least, was a custom he could still honor. He pulled out a piece of the dried fish, then closed the bag and arranged it behind himself, to make a pillow of sorts. The planks had never felt hard before—perhaps this was just age; perhaps it was that he was not used to sitting for so long. He leaned forward, making an involuntary grunt as his legs took the weight again, and slid the bag under the seat of his pants. There was a cracking sound as he settled back onto the bag, a flash of recognition and a pang of disappointment. His pipe. There was still tobacco, and he would have liked to smoke the pipe after eating. He had never been a man of many vices, and he found that tobacco often helped him gather his thoughts. It would have been nice to gather his thoughts there, one last time, before he died.

Never mind—it might still be of use; he would find out later. For now, he would sit and eat.

He pulled at strips of the dried fish, placing each on his tongue and letting the memories drawn from smoke and salt and oil fill his mind. How was it that Jewel, who never truly had a mother, knew so well how to prepare fish? It is made with a daughter's love, she would say—that was her recipe, and he knew not to ask any more. A daughter's love was a powerful thing, he knew; almost—he thought—as strong as a father's. And which of those two was it that had kept him alive for so long?

Yes, Jewel had seemed to learn everything by herself. She was as smart as her mother that way. His friends had tried to warn him away from her mother, back in Ziah, when they were young. Nyonontee is too smart for you, they said, she's too smart for anyone. You marry her, and you'll be at the fire cooking up cassava while she sits in your chair smoking the pipe! He knew better: a smart woman knows how to take care of her man. And she *was* strong, too. Who cared if she frightened the other men? They wanted wives they could cow and beat—women who would be helpless without them. A woman like Nyonontee was not to be won by beating.

It was at the market in Ziah that the old man had first spoken to her. He was young, but fully grown, and handsome then—and had come for market day with Virgil and Marcus to bring back rugs their mother purchased the week before. The brothers saw the girl and called out to her. Oh, these are too heavy for a man, Nyonontee—come, carry them for us!

The old man was embarrassed by their rudeness; he called out to her on his own in mock supplication: Please don't embarrass them by showing how weak they are, he said. If you do, we'll never find husbands for them.

She laughed a full-bodied laugh, not even bothering to hide those beautiful straight white teeth with her hands. Two weeks later, he went to Garley's village and introduced himself to her father.

He was done with the fish now, and considered retrieving his bag for another piece. No, that would mean standing again, and his legs rebelled at the thought. He would sit here a while longer and bask in the warmth of the day.

Yes, he had chosen well when he married... but the birds went silent again; there was a motorbike coming. From the direction of Ziah this time. If he closed his eyes, he could feel its approach by weighing the sound: now it was slowing by the stream, now climbing the path just beyond the rise of the hill; left, then right—if he turned his head, he would see it in a few moments. How was it, that with all that had left him—his strength, his sight, his family—that his hearing was as sharp as ever?

When he was young he would lie there in the forest clearing, away from the water, and listen with his eyes closed. The water hid everything, but if he was far enough from the water and the wind was not up, he believed that he could see the forest in his head as well as if he were looking with his eyes. Here were mice, hollowing out a new burrow, and there was the banana palm swaying heavy under its fruit. They would be ripe and good to eat soon, he knew. And the footsteps coming, slowly, down the path? His brother, in no obvious hurry to retrieve him and return to the task of hoeing the new field for corn.

The motorbike had crested the hill now and was coming down it, toward him, slowing. He recognized the man on the front but did not know his name. The man was often on the road, bringing people to the clinic in Ziah, bringing medicine to the villages.

There was a stranger on the back of the motorbike, a young man who looked neither black nor white. This must be the Indian doctor, he thought. There had been plenty of talk about the Indian doctor these past couple of years, of how he was teaching the villages to do their own medicine, and telling them to bring their sick to Ziah when that was not enough. How he spoke Bassa and Krahn and called Liberia his home. They said he was born here, and left during the war. But he left to go to America and become a doctor, and now he had come back.

The man from the clinic called a greeting as he rolled the bike to a stop. Good afternoon, Grandfather! *Ku merie?* How are you today?

He welcomed them and said he was well enough.

The driver introduced himself as Horace, said he was from the clinic, and this was Doctor Raj. The doctor introduced himself as well—his Krahn was not good, but his eyes were clear and kind. He shook the old man's hand in the traditional style. Are you sure you are feeling well, he asked.

Well enough, the old man repeated.

Mrs. Charity from Bilibo had come to the clinic and told us she was worried about you. She said you thought you were dying.

The old man thought on this in silence for a few moments. He was not sure this was a matter for doctors. He shook his head and smiled. No, no—my health is fine.

The doctor sat by him and held his hand; he was gentle, this doctor. Would you mind if we sat with you a while? I would like to make sure of your health.

That would be fine. The old man would not mind having company for a little while.

You live alone here? the doctor asked.

With my daughter, said the old man, but she has been gone now for a while. Do you know of her? Her name is Jewel. He told of how she had gone to Ziah, and how he had waited for her return.

The doctor said he did not know her, but knew people who could help look. He would speak to them when he returned to Zwedru that evening. Would that be all right? Yes, the old man said, and for a moment felt his hand on something, something like the heavy lid of a box that he might try to open. The possibility that his Jewel might yet be found, that she might still come back to him. No, he said—but only to himself— he did not want his heart to feel that loss again, and let his hand rest where it was. But to the doctor he said yes again. Yes, that would be fine.

Grandfather, the doctor said to him, may I listen to your heart? That would also be fine, the old man said, and he breathed slowly while the earnest young man laid his small metal disk against the old man's chest and closed his eyes, seeming to be very far away in thought.

Your heart is strong, the doctor said. The old man thought a while, thinking of what he might tell the doctor of his heart, thinking of what he might ask. In the end he only said yes—yes it is.

Have you eaten today? Yes, said the old man again, and pulled at his bag to offer the two visitors some of his fish. He was not in Gbagee, but suddenly felt embarrassed at not having given them the hospitality that was due a guest. No, thank you, they said, we have eaten well, and the three men sat in comfortable silence as the finches squabbled overhead.

Grandfather, said Horace after a while, we must go now, Doctor Raj and I. But tomorrow I will return. There are things I must take to Bilibo. If you wish, I can bring you things too—some food, medicine. Horace and the doctor looked at each other, exchanging words without speaking, then he continued. If you wish, Grandfather, I could bring you back to Ziah when I return. You could stay with us a few days while we look for your daughter. Would you like me to do this?

The sun had moved to the west now, coaxing the first traces of a breeze from the sweltering forest. There was a thickness in the air as it came, and the old man took it into his lungs and let it rest there. It felt like rain, and the old man thought a little rain would not be a bad thing on a day as hot and still as this. But the rains had left for the year, and the billowing clouds he could see beyond the tops of the trees might provide a little shade as they passed, but would bring no water.

Grandfather? And the old man realized he had not answered, but the time had passed, and he no longer remembered what the young man had asked him. Yes, he said, as a question, and the young man asked again: tomorrow, when I come—would you like me to take you with me, back to Ziah?

No, the old man said. No, you are very kind, but I must stay here, in case my Jewel returns. She would not know what to do if I were not here when she came home. He did not like to lie, not to these earnest young men. But they would not understand. The young do not understand death the same way the old do; they believe it is something you must always fight, or run from, like a snake.

The young doctor stood and held his hand again, and thanked the old man for welcoming them. Horace had started his motorbike—sputtering first, then erupting in a cloud of blue smoke; he lifted his helmet as the doctor climbed on. I will see you tomorrow then, Grandfather? he asked, and the old man bowed his head, seeming to agree, but saying nothing as they rode away.

There was a gentle but steady breeze now, and even after the noise of the motorbike had faded over the hills to the west, the sounds of the forest were muted, lost in thousand whispers of wind moving through the tree tops. This was a good time of day, the old man thought, when the heat has passed and there is no more work to do. He pulled again at the bag, settling himself back onto the bare wood, and retrieved the pieces of the broken pipe. The stem had snapped near the base, but it was a clean break, and he imagined that he could hold the two pieces together as he smoked. He tore a piece of tobacco from the wad in his pocket and rolled it between his fingers, letting the dry brown shreds fill the pipe's clay bowl before tamping them down with his thumb. He brought his hand to his nose and breathed in slowly; it was old tobacco, but he had kept it dry in a fold of plastic, and the sharp, earthy smell of it on his fingers pleased him.

And the matches? Yes, there were plenty—he sorted through a few of the candidates he kept in the fold of the plastic and selected one with a straight shaft and unchipped head. He held it up to the afternoon light, rotating it in his fingers as though it was an important thing, knowing it was not, but still taking pleasure in the exercise.

He worried that he was too clumsy to strike the match and hold his pipe together at the same time; he would have to set the match down to take up the two pieces. He practiced the motion once, twice, then discarded it as impractical—he would simply hold the bowl and draw from where the stem had broken off until it was fully lit.

The match flared and he held the bowl to his lips, pursing and puffing, imagining the picture he must make doing so, glad there was no one to see him like this. But the tobacco caught and once he was able to fit the stem in place, he found he could hold it there with one hand. He watched the smoke rise and curl from the glowing embers in the bowl, then vanish as the wind caught it. He did not want to rush this moment, and found that just holding the pipe there, watching its patient tendrils of smoke, calmed him and helped him gather his thoughts.

No, his life had not been easy, not since Charles Taylor, not since he had buried James, the boy. And not since Jewel, his Jewel, his wife's last gift, had left for the Ziahtown market two weeks ago. But there had been good years, many of them, before that. He closed his eyes and saw himself, still a boy, chasing Virgil and Marcus through the brush, felt himself lying on his back against the warm flat rock by the clearing, listening to the forest speak to him. He saw himself riding on his grandfather's shoulders, saying, Tell me another story—another! And he saw himself fully grown, and his wife, round and glowing with child, watching proudly as he told his own stories to the children around the fire. He held these memories in his left hand and hefted them, feeling their weight. Then he drew slowly from the pipe and felt the warm comfort of the smoke settle in his lungs. How was one supposed to weigh these good years against the bad?

A ghost of self-pity rose up in him, objecting—had not everything he worked for come to nothing? The old man blew the smoke in its face, silenced it like a spoiled child. In the end, we all come to nothing, he said. Why should you expect to be any different? Yes, he had lost James and had lost Jewel. But what if he had never even known the boy? Never watched his youngest daughter grow to be a woman? It was a stupid game to play, pretending you could place them on a balance and ask which had counted for more. Even in this one short day there had been good and bad.

He drew in another lungful from his pipe. It was working, he thought, this trick of holding the stem and bowl together with his fingers. He examined the fracture more closely—it would be simple to fix with a little clay; he could join the pieces cleanly, and nothing would betray the break except a thin brown line. His sudden laugh surprised him, and he gagged for a moment on the smoke—he had not laughed in a very long time. Then he settled himself again, and watched the last embers of the tobacco dwindle and go out.

There was more tobacco in his pocket, he knew, but did not feel the need to smoke it now. It had served its purpose, helped him gather his thoughts. Now, he supposed, there was nothing to do but close his eyes and wait.

He heard her voice calling him and he looked up along the direction that led to Ziahtown. She had called to him in Krahn, calling him father, and using his old name, not the Christian one. And then he saw her as she came down the path, his Jewel, holding her hands out for him. She was sorry she had come back from market so late; she hoped he had not been waiting long. He saw that her dress was new and clean and beautiful—where had she found money for it? There was cloth, too, and sandals and baskets. He had so many questions—where were you so many days? How have you bought these things? But she hushed him and said it was late, and he must be hungry, and we must not keep mother waiting. And she took him by the hand and took the baskets and cloth on her head and led him back through the forest path that left the road.

With her holding his hand, he was no longer tired as he walked. His knee felt strong when he placed his weight on it. Ahead, he heard the sound of his brother's hatchet, hewing timber for the new palava. It would be good to have a new palava. And beyond, singing. The boys singing—"*Tokay Tomeh Kailie...*" and the crack of a stick slapped on the ground to hold the rhythm. They played like that when they were younger; it was good to hear them play again. As he entered the clearing, there was woodsmoke, and the smell of meat being grilled. How long it had been since his wife had cooked meat—this must be a special day that he had forgotten.

His eldest daughter saw him first from the mud-brick cooking hut and called out to James that his grandfather had returned. When the boy came running, his eyes were filled with light and laughter, and the old man lifted him up, up onto his shoulders and was surprised that he could carry James so easily.

The boy drummed his hands on the old man's head and squealed in delight while his daughter scolded him and told him to be gentle. She took his other hand, so he was walking along the path with one daughter in each hand and his grandson on his shoulders.

And then he heard his wife calling from inside the bungalow—You've brought him at last, that man always makes me wait for him!—and there were footsteps as the boys came, tall and strong as they always were, and they held their hands out for him and brought his chair and tobacco and asked him to sit. And when he did, they sat around him on the floor, eager and patient at once while he poured the tobacco and lit his pipe. And when he breathed it in, he was very tired all at once, and called to his wife, and she came to him and rested his head on her shoulder and sang softly until he closed his eyes and slept.

Fly Away

Forward and back, forward and back. The brief rush of wind in her face sweeps her hair away; centrifugal force pushes her down in the seat, then flings her upward toward the house, toward the sky, where for a moment she is weightless, suspended. Then gravity renews its tug and again the wind comes, now from behind, as she plunges backward towards the ground, gripping the steel chains of the swing like twin rosaries. Her dusty blue Skechers make a brief chirp! as they scuff well-worn grooves beneath her feet, and again she's up, this time among the yew trees, looking down at the old trampled ferns. Then weightless, free for another brief moment before plunging to earth one more time. Forward and back, forward and back.

She thinks: This will now be "the old house"—that's what her mother always called the one they'd left in California eleven years ago. What will she call it now that they're moving back? Will this become "the old Pittsburgh house"? Up until now it had just been "the house"—the house on the corner, the one with cracked stucco and old timbers. The house where, when it rained hard, kids squeezed up onto the sheltered porch until the school bus came. If it were really cold, sometimes her mother would come out with a pot of hot cocoa and a stack of miniature Dixie cups. Of course the other parents never minded, not like in California, where there'd be forms to sign and questions about hygiene and nut allergies. She tells people she remembers California, but really she thinks she just remembers her parents' stories of what it was like. She'll find out soon enough.

Her father had hung the swing when she was much younger; back then she had to stand on tiptoes and yank herself up by the chains to slide into the soft rubber seat. "Push me, daddy! Push me!" And he would. Sometimes one-handed, absentmindedly while looking up, out to the house, the sky, somewhere far away. Sometimes he would take both hands to the chains and pretend he was launching her into space. Gripping, pushing her higher, higher each time, until he came running, clear under the swing from behind to pop out in front, gaping in mock astonishment at finding himself in the little yard behind the house on the corner. She thinks back, and tries to remember the last time she asked for a push.

Of course, she is much too big for the swing now—swings like this were meant for little kids—but it still gives her comfort, and as she's grown, so have the twin grooves beneath her feet. Forward and back, forward and back, with each little chirp! at the bottom taking another small measure out of dirt and the soles of her too-recently-new shoes. Each time, the renewed momentum feeding some unnamed longing, just for a moment, as it flings her out into space again.

Ella. She does remember Ella—she's certain of that. They'd been inseparable once, before Ella's parents moved away for some university job. But that was so long ago; it was when she still believed in wishes, and her father had helped her tie a note to a balloon saying "Will you be my friend? Signed, Katherine."

They launched it from the back yard, right over there. Since she still believed in wishes, it was only natural that Ella wrote back from Virginia, saying she'd found the note on a balloon stuck in the tree in her own back yard. She thinks she'd be happier if she still believed in wishes.

But Ella is two people now, she thinks—the one she knows, frozen on the dresser mirror in a third-grade school photo, impish grin under neatly trimmed bangs. The other one, maybe in Virginia, maybe moved on yet again. Fifteen, like herself, and grown into a woman.

She wonders if she will be like this to the friends she leaves behind here. How she will grow and change, but the Cerniaks and the Butlers next door will preserve this Katherine, always fifteen, moody and bookish, reticent and kind. At least she hopes she'll be remembered as kind. But how strange to still be this person to them, to leave a ghost of herself behind when she goes. She's not sure she likes the idea, but then, she never did like the idea of leaving in the first place. Maybe this is the magic of the swing, always going, always coming back.

The swing used to make more noise when her father first put it up. He'd picked it up at a rummage sale and bought a couple of eye bolts and carabiners at Home Depot to hang it from the arbor. It looked simple enough, and made a reassuring creak as she swung. Forward—creak!—and back. Forward—creak!—and back. Two years ago, one of the carabiners gave way at the bottom of the arc and launched her backwards into the ferns.

Her father showed her the torn piece of metal. The constant rhythm of steel chain over the years had worn right through the lower end of the failed ring. They went out the next weekend and bought proper mounting hardware, and she'd climbed the ladder to help him attach it. Now the chain was silent as she swung, and there was only the wind, and a brief chirp! each time her shoes punished the uncomplaining earth beneath her feet.

Someone else would be living in this house, she thought. Maybe, if they had a girl, she'd swing on this swing, too. She might wonder about the grooves. Maybe her father would fill them in, or pay someone to do that. Or maybe they'd just take the swing down, and it would exist only in her memory, a companion to the ghost of her own memory that would remain here.

They'd paint her room, of course. Her mother had loved that color of yellow—so bright, so real and warm she could hold it and squeeze it in her hand like the lemons they bought Sundays at the farmers market. When they'd put drop cloth down and opened up the first can of paint, the dripping yellow on the roller looked like magic. Her father let her paint all over the walls with that roller, and she spelled her name in letters two feet high: K-A-T-H-E-R-I-N-E. She'd run out of room on the first wall and had to put the "INE" on the one across the doorway. It felt like power, like magic in her hands. It was like she was casting a spell on the room to make it her own. And even though her father had dipped the roller again after she was done and painted everything over into a smooth bright finish, her name, and the spell remained hidden beneath. Whenever she lay in bed and looked at those bright yellow walls she felt the warmth of summer, of the farmers market and the smell of fresh lemons in her hand.

The October wind has blown leaves from the giant oak through the back yard—no reason for anyone to rake them now, she supposes. A few have encroached on the edges of the packed dirt under the swing, and she stretches one foot to reach them. Forward—chirp-swish!—and back, forward—chirp-swish!—and back. She waits for more leaves, but the wind has settled again, and now it's only her motion that produces the sound, and the breeze on her face.

She muses at how time works, at how she is waiting. Waiting for more leaves to come. Waiting for her father to call to her. She would like to save up some of this waiting, to gather it up in a bag or a little bottle. She would like to place it among her keepsakes in the pink jewelry box Nana gave her when she was very small. There was a clockwork on the box, and if you kept the spring wound up, a little plastic ballerina popped up and turned slowly when you opened it. She used to love the box for the dancing ballerina, but now she loves it for the sad feeling it gives her. It contains the memories of things she's tried to hold on to. The worry stone from Auntie Jill, the old coins, unspent tokens from Chuck E. Cheese. The cheap thermal photo from the arcade of her and…why could she not remember the girl's name? She was sure they'd be best friends forever, after Ella left. And now? The nameless girl in the picture wasn't even a memory anymore—just a faded ghost of a memory that had once been a friend.

The pink box is already far away; she'd placed it under her raincoat and the shiny green duck boots that were already too small for her in one of the brown cardboard crates her parents had left in her room on packing day. She'd slept in a sleeping bag on her old bed the last night and found herself crying at the thought of being a stranger in her own house. But there were no tears now, just the rhythm of the wind and gravity, and the sure pumping of her legs keeping the swing flying through space: forward and back, forward and back.

She remembers how, when they'd traveled to Seattle that one time, her father insisted on stopping by the house where he had grown up. He knocked and explained who he was, and asked if they could come in to look. The woman made them licorice tea and set out a tray of cookies while her father pointed at rooms and windows and the back porch, saying "Oh, look—here? When I was seven, I took my mum's best sheets out and glued them to the railing to make a circus tent!"

She imagines herself years from now, with a husband and children of her own, coming back to this place, back to the old Pittsburgh house and knocking on the door. See, there? That was my room—when I was young, we painted it bright yellow, and my father let me write my name on the wall it in letters two feet high. And out back? You see where that orange tree is? We used to have an arbor there, with a swing hung under it...

Forward and back, forward and back. The rush downward, then up into the sky, hanging there momentarily until gravity renews its tug and pulls her down, back, the rush of wind in her hair and the world is full of trees and ferns. Forward and back, forward and back. Then a voice from the steps: "Katherine? You ready? It's time." She feels the downward rush one last time, a final chirp! at the bottom as the swing launches her ahead, upward and into the sky as she lets go of the chains and flies away.

Jaguar

The man on the bus said he had to tell me. I figured he just had to tell anyone who would listen. I figured that, as the only gringo within a hundred miles, I was an obvious target. Back home, I was always the guy who the lonely, the crazies, the ones who just needed to talk —I was always the one they singled out of the crowd. I'd shield my eyes, lose myself in a book, whatever. It didn't matter.

"*Hombre.*"

I felt him push in. The old grandmother and her impassable woven sack of—what were they?—nuts or whatever, shooed him away like a fly, but he pushed in. There simply wasn't enough room there on the bench seat. Not between me, pack on my lap, the old lady, her sacks and the *niño* slung at her side. There wasn't room anywhere, but it seems to be an axiom of these rusted old mountain buses that there's always room for one more. And so there he was, at my side, whispering into my ear.

"*Hey hombre — Americano?*"

I ignored him, pressing my face to the window, watching—feeling, really—the dense green foliage wash over my eyes. Below our feet the wheels crawled, uncertainly, up rutted dirt road through the jungle of the valley floor. It would be another four hours before we rose from the crease of this valley into the breathtaking, heart-stopping switchbacks that would take us over the pass, down into the next. And from there another four, assuming the engine held and we didn't blow another tire.

"Hombre — please. You American? You speak English? I have to tell you something."

The grandmother scolded him in — probably in Imwa—and he dismissed her with an unfamiliar flight of words, almost whistled under his breath. Then his hand was on my shoulder, and I could feel his breath, heavy with some spice, at the back of my ear.

"Please — just listen."

Did I have any choice? I rested my head against my pack, facing away from him, and fingered the carved hummingbird totem dangling from its strap. It was going to be a long ride.

It was many years ago, the man said, before his father's father was born. Back then, they still hunted the jaguar. It wasn't for meat, not like the Imwa, but for the spirit. He wasn't Imwa—they didn't know the power of animal spirits, he said. He was—I didn't catch the name—it might have been "Quetla," but the word itself sounded as though it were two notes from a song. The Quetla knew how to use animals, he said. Before planting, you needed to catch opossum—their spirit knew the ways of the earth, of seeds. You had to catch it, alive, and bring it to your field. There, you asked its help, and with a stone knife cut from the earth, you drained its blood into the ground. Then, to remind the earth of the opossum's gift, you wore its skin while you tilled and planted. For safety in childbirth, you caught the howler monkey; for fever, the river caiman—this was the way it was. In times of drought, the crane. And in times of war, the jaguar.

Back then, there was a war, or there was going to be one. The Imwa—I could now hear the note of derision in his voice when he said the name—had a bad harvest, and were blaming the Quetla, blaming their magic. The Quetla mostly kept to themselves, and it had been generations since they'd had any need to fight. But they held a council, and decided they needed a warrior. They chose a man who lived at the edge of the village. A farmer.

"Why?"

The sound of the word in my mouth surprised me. I still hadn't looked at him, this man whispering in my ear. I'd kept my face to the window, eyes lost in the dark swirling stream of jungle as it eddied past us. I had pretended I wasn't listening, pretended he wasn't even there. But then I said it: "Why?"

"Why what?"

"Why a farmer?"

"Ah, it's a very good question." He paused, and seemed to savor it. I pressed my face harder against the glass, as if disavowing my participation in the story. Really, I had no idea why I'd asked. Maybe to trip him up?

"They picked him because of the ants."

"Ah—obviously." But I should have known better: sarcasm is never a good idea outside of one's own culture.

His voice took a tone of pleasant surprise: "You know these things?"

"No."

He held his disappointment and went on: this man, the farmer, had not asked to be a warrior; one didn't ask for these things. But he, like all the Quetla, obeyed the signs of the animals. He didn't have a wife, so the grandmothers of the village prepared him, sewing the colors to his clothes and drying the strips of meat for his journey. A hunter must become the animal he hunts, so the man would become the jaguar, dressing as it did, eating what it ate.

After three days, he set out, armed with rope, machete, bow, and the short, wide-feathered Quetla arrows. Oh yes: and the stone knife. The trick, remember, was not to kill the jaguar—that would bring him nothing. He had to catch it alive and ask for its help. Only then could he cut its throat with the stone knife, paint himself with its blood and wear its skin. Only in this way could he become a warrior and save his people.

"So he was a hunter."

"No, no. Maybe a little. Monkeys, wild pigs. But no. He was a farmer."

"Jesus."

He paused, perhaps considering the intent of the religious invocation.

It took four days, following the river up stream, before the man first heard the jaguar's cry. It doesn't sound like a cat, they say. It sounds like a woman, a woman crying out in anguish, and it's not something you can forget.

In the jungle, it's even worse: sound reflects off of everything—you can't really tell where it's coming from. All you hear is the cry, the anguished cry, coming from everywhere at once. So the man following the river. By day he walked; by night, he laid snares and rubbed the blood of a goat into the dirt of his path before tying his hammock and trying to sleep.

One of the old Quetla had told him what to do: a jaguar lives in the trees, but its prey lives on the ground. So he too must sleep high among the trees like the jaguar, not low to the ground like its prey.

Each night after that first, he heard the jaguar's cry, and each night it sounded closer. There among the branches, his dreams circled in on themselves: was he a man hunting a jaguar, or a jaguar, hunting the man? He felt his feet, silent on the wet carpet of leaves, his nose tracing an unfamiliar scent. And when the cries woke him, he could not be sure they weren't his own screams.

It was on the fifth day that he reached that place on the side of the mountain where the canopy fell away into open ground. It wasn't a place for a jaguar, not there, on the rough bare slope of the volcano without any cover. It wasn't a place for him, either, but each had led the other here.

He climbed until night fell, purple clouds shrouding the earth below him, and knew he had left the world of the living. It was not natural to see these things from above, from this far away. Such a view was only for the gods, and for the spirits who had already served their time among men.

There were no trees here from which to hang his hammock, so he laid it out on a ledge, a blade of red stone jutting from the face of the mountain like a knife that had been thrust into the earth and left there. He had never understood the cold, and it was cold here. He knew the dead were cold, and wondered if this was what it felt like to be dead. This made him afraid—he did not like the idea of being so cold forever.

But he reminded himself why he was here. He'd painted the trail of blood and set out his snare as best he could on the rock, covering it with what little loose dirt he could find. Then he lay down to wait. And when the moonless sky sunk into blackness, the stars lifted him away, into space.

His mother had taught him the constellations: the badger, the crocodile. The great river, the hunter. And yes, the jaguar. As a child, he and his brother had gone to the clearings at night and looked up to the sky. Then it was so far away; now, it enveloped him, wrapped him in its light like a blanket. He could see the river flow, watched as the crocodile snuck up on the foolish monkey at its bank. He looked down at the earth and saw that he was now the hunter, moving among the other constellations, and there, always just out of his reach, was the jaguar. He heard its cry and even there, among the stars, its voice came from everywhere at once.

Or was that his cry? Looking over his shoulder, as the jaguar in the sky did, he saw the hunter pursuing him. They both ran, moving effortlessly over the rough ground below and somehow, at the same time, through the stars above. His breath came hot and sharp, yet he ran on, until he no longer knew whether he was the pursuer or the pursued, knowing only that the distance between them would not close. It was then that he called out and, hearing his own voice come from behind, turned and crouched, waiting for that next moment when...

The two of them fell, tangled and snarling, from the ledge and into the earth below.

"And?"

He'd stopped talking, the sorrow in his eyes giving a finality to the story. I had turned to face him—I don't know when—but his eyes were not on me. They were somewhere far away, lost in melancholy amid the dark wash of jungle outside our dirty window.

I tried again: "And?"

"And what?"

"And what happened next?"

"Nothing happened next."

The Quetla must have waited until the end for their warrior to return, reading what signs they could from the ants and dragonflies. They were no match for the Imwa when they came, and their blood joined that of the opossum in the ground. The valley was all Imwa now, and their own legends erased any memory that another people once lived here among them.

A weary sadness had descended upon him, and I could not bring myself to ask any more questions. We sat in silence, the window reflecting our eyes, reflecting the now-thinning green as we reached the pass that would lead us down into the next valley. The bus shuddered to a halt where a clot of thatch-roofed huts cowered into the mountain saddle, and there was the noise of people climbing over each other, retrieving their packages, to get off, to get on. When I looked back in, he'd moved away, a greasy leather bedroll slung over his shoulder as he straddled the chicken crates and sleeping children between me and the door.

I called out to him, "Hey!" and he turned. "How— how do you even know that story?"

He looked puzzled.

"I have always known it."

Then he was turning away again, and I grasped for something, anything. "And why me? Why did you say you needed to tell me?"

When he turned back, he met my eyes, and I saw for the first time that his were not black like the others. They were a pale green. The color of the jungle. The color of something else I only half remembered.

"Because you also tell stories. Because you will take this one with you and tell it to others."

"How...?"

He smiled.

"Because of the hummingbird."

And then he was gone, out the door.

The hummingbird. It had been given to me by an old woman in the marketplace. I never knew her name, but since the first day I'd wandered into that tangled maze of stalls, I'd made a habit of stopping and talking with her. She knitted hats, and I wanted a hat. She spoke no English, of course, but was patient with my broken Spanish and tutored me, day after day, in what little small talk we could share. She asked about my home, my family, my travels, and I told her stories of them all. By the end of the third week, I had a dozen hats I didn't need, but my Spanish had never been better.

At the end of the month, when I told her it was time for me to go, she brought out a polished wooden box. It was inlaid with metal in the shapes of animals— crocodiles and monkeys, ants and dragonflies. She rummaged through the coins and colored stones inside and brought out a carved hummingbird, gray wings, white head and a chest as improbably green as her eyes. Yes, I'd forgotten about her eyes. That's what made me stop and talk with her in the first place. A gringo in the market is like fresh meat, after all—every hand on your shoulder, pulling, come, come see what I have for you. No, don't listen to that old fool, he's got nothing but trash. Here, a poncho for you. A nice bag for your señorita. Come, come.

But she sat quietly among her hats, that ancient woman, watching me with those eyes. Because she did not call out to me, I went to her. A month later, when it was time to leave, she tied the hummingbird to my pack.

"Un regalo," she said, *"para recordarnos"*—a gift to remember us by. *Us.* Then she added something else, whispered words of an almost whistling language I didn't recognize.

My fingers traced the outline of the small carved bird now, a talisman in my hand. Green like the jungle in the valley below. Green like the eyes of a jaguar. As the bus lurched back into motion, I pressed my face to the window one last time, watching the man who had given me this new story to tell. Watching as he climbed, alone, up the bare rocky slope, where high above, a blade of red stone jutted from the mountainside like a knife.

Last Night Ashore

All anyone's looking for is love—that's what it said at
the bottom of the note. It took me a moment to place it,
but then I remembered: it was almost the same thing
he'd said coming out of Santino's, that last night
ashore. It didn't mean a damned thing at the time—
why should it? Jason said all sorts of crazy shit. But
seeing those same words there on the note.... Well, I
guess it gave me pause.

He was halfway through the door when he'd said it.
Halfway through when he saw the two strays lingering
in the drizzle there at the top of the steps. Lingering
like they were waiting for their owner, like they knew
he'd return any minute from his weekly rendezvous
with the redhead who tended bar at Santino's on
Friday nights.

Of course, they didn't have an owner—none of the
dogs of Punta Arenas did. None except those dainties
you'd see out on leash along the windswept coastal
promenade, indifferent to the indignities of their knit
pink doggie vests and—if it happened to be some
holiday—a poodle-sized gaucho hat riding over one
floppy ear.

No, I'd always thought of the dogs around Punta
Arenas as some sort of community property: happy to
call any man master for a midnight walk and a scratch
behind the ear. If they wanted anything more, they
took pains not to show it. They would wait for anyone,
but that night, for Jason, they were waiting for him. He

was halfway through the door when he saw them, a wagtail golden lab and her mutt companion, and he dropped to his knees so quickly that I nearly went clean over his back.

He'd been drinking, of course; we all had, but Jason seemed to have gotten an earlier start than the rest of us, and it brought out a sort of melancholy in him that was unbecoming in a man of his physical presence.

We'd been in port four days then. Jason was rotating in, and I was part of the turnaround from the last cruise, offloading the old team of beakers and bringing the new ones on. It had been a fine cruise—I'd served with worse—but it was good to have solid ground under my feet, whiskey in my belly and the prospect of a shapely Latina on my arm. Here in Punta Arenas, there was at least a chance of finding a woman who was interested in more than titration, turbidity, and zooplankton lipids.

Alas, I was a wiry kid back then, and the ladies of PA didn't seem to be into "wiry," eloquence be damned. Still I couldn't complain: the icebreaker was a good gig. Good captain, good crew, and a solid hull beneath us. A hell of a lot safer than the boats I'd worked out of Cordova, longlining on the Gulf in all sorts of shit weather. We never knew whether we'd get our asses back in one piece, let alone have anything to show for it. Four seasons down here, and I still had fewer scars from the Drake than from my one year in Alaska.

And you could pick worse places than Punta Arenas for a turnaround. It was an island town of sorts, cut off from Mother Chile by a swoop of the southern Andes. Sure, windswept and cold as hell, but relaxed and friendly. Charming, even. If all else failed, there was always company to be had from the fine ladies out on Republica.

But the program didn't choose PA for its charm or its ladies; it was just the cheapest and fastest place to turn a ship like this around. They gave us just four days to do it each time: four days to unload and reload, to fuel and stock and staff for yet another month-long foray, supporting whatever crazy Antarctic science this latest batch of beakers had signed up for. We spent the days on the pier in a blur of manifest sheets and crates of god-knows-what, constantly interrupted by some junior PI looking for the MPC, or yet another grad student trying to find his way to aft control. And the nights? We spent the nights in town.

Most of us tended to eat on board before wandering down to the bar at Hotel Cabo. The service there was lousy, but it was a good place to start the evening: you could pull a bunch of tables together in front of the fireplace so any number of people could sit and drink while arguing over where to go next. La Luna? Los Ganadores? Or maybe down the waterfront to the casino, where there was rumor of some band playing at midnight.

It was clear that the staff at Cabo had come to expect our visitations whenever the ship was in port, and I don't think they minded: we tended to tip well, and were probably a refreshing break from their usual clientele. The new team usually stayed at Cabo, too, before they came on board. So starting at the bar there was a chance to mingle and get introduced on neutral ground. There were always plenty of introductions to be made: for every old hand back from last year's krill survey or seismic mapping, there'd be two or three eager new kids in tow, breathless grad students bouncing off the bulkhead at the thought of their first ice. No, we didn't call them "fingies"—not on this ship. It was always good to have new kids aboard. Sure, they could get tiresome, but mostly they'd just make you smile, and you'd say, Yeah, I remember my first time. If nothing else, they helped you remember.

So we'd be sitting, drinking, trying to keep names straight while putting in an offhand vote to hit La Marmita for a second round of dinner. Then Jason would slide in, quietly, and take a seat by the rail in the corner, and a cheer would go up at the return of another familiar face. "Hey—they promised me you weren't coming back," and "I thought that buffalo grass hooch was supposed to kill you." Of course, we were all bullshitting—Jason was sullen, but there wasn't a soul who wasn't glad to sail with him. Then someone would ask what he was drinking and he'd shrug noncommittally. One of the Latin women would plant herself maternally in his ample lap and foist a pisco sour on him, and conversation would go on as before.

Eventually, word would percolate that a decision had been made: Emilio wanted to go to Mesita Grande, damn it, so we were going to Mesita Grande. How many? Ten, twelve—just get us the big table, and we'll be along as soon as we finished our beer.

Mesita Grande was where we went that night, our last night ashore. It was still a month before spring, and the weather dithered nightly between snow and rain. I volunteered to go with the first group, out into the plaza with my collar up—left or right?—it didn't matter from here, drifting down Pedro Montt towards the waterfront, down toward the glittering, enticing windows of restaurant alley with the obligatory dog or two in tow from the moment we left the steps at Cabo.

As a Marine Tech, you had to be at least a little social: whenever any gear needed to go over the side— a krill tow, a CTD drop, whatever—you had to work with whoever owned the damned thing to make sure it was done the way they wanted. But there were also long hours alone, and Jason seemed to like it that way. You could catch him out on the back deck, up against the rail, watching the water go by, endless, impossibly cold and dark. You could check back in half an hour later and, if he'd not been needed elsewhere, he might still be standing in the same spot. Mind you, he was always amenable to company; he'd give you a nod if you sidled up beside him to look over the stern. But if you wanted conversation, you were going to have to be the one to start it.

"Thinking about a swim?"

He watched the sea, impenetrable and unanswering, for a minute before he spoke.

"You know," he said, "I've heard this thing about fear of heights."

"Yeah?" I waited, and he mulled the rest over, deciding how to proceed.

"The way I understand it, it's not a fear that you're going to fall. It's a fear that you're not going to be able to prevent yourself from jumping."

I told him he was scaring me.

"Don't worry. It would be a shitty way to go. And you guys would be down a Marine Tech." Then he got that sideways smirk on his face and said, "But I might be tempted to push Andy."

Oh God, Andy. Yeah, I promised I'd help.

We were all on a second round of pizza, and the empty Austral bottles were piling up by the time Daniela pulled Jason in through the swinging doors of Mesita Grande, tugging him along like a reluctant man-child.

"You saved some for us, I hope?" And she shooed a couple of the new kids far enough along the bench to make room for the two of them. I don't think Jason particularly liked that kind of attention, but he didn't protest too loudly. As I said, the Latin girls tended to adopt him, and the mothering gave him some sort of plausible deniability about why he was there. Besides, on the last night there was a sort of unspoken rule about at least making a good show of things before heading back to the ship. Even Hank had joined in the fun.

So we plied Jason with pizza and cheap local beer, and by the time there was a move to head somewhere "with real drinks" he seemed loose enough in his clothes to come along without complaint.

The bar that night was Santino's, a somber, wood-paneled lounge a couple of blocks up Avenida Colón. It was more swank than the Colonial, like it was trying to lean in on the look and feel of the grand old taverns that lined the plaza to the south. We were down to eight, and when Daniela returned from a trip to the loo, she planted herself on an armrest of the leather couch with the two new students from Scripps, recasting our little peninsula of lounge chairs into an archipelago.

For some reason, we were all drinking Calafate then, and Jason stared into the deep blue of his drink with the same patience I remembered from those nights out on the rail at sea.

"You about ready?" I had no idea whether I was talking about setting out on the cruise, calling it an evening or just throwing back the prim champagne glass that seemed to have transfixed him. I guess I was a little annoyed at finding myself on social babysitting duty my last night ashore.

He thought about my question for a minute— maybe he was trying to figure it out, too. He twirled the stem of his drink slowly there on the table. Then, "You know?" It was that same voice from the back deck. "Last time I was up in Torres, I met a girl."

Her name was Carolina, and she spoke as little English as he spoke Spanish. He'd missed the afternoon bus back and found himself wandering some dirt trail in the broad river valley to pass the unexpected day. He was stopped at an inconclusive fork in the road, trying to decide whether he had any reason to choose one over the other, when he heard steps behind him, the sound of feet ambling on gravel. She paused and smiled, the way you would to a stranger on some small town street corner, then nodded her head to the left. *"Por aquí"*—this way.

They made a brief fitful attempt at conversation: *"No Español? No Português? Lo siento…"* She didn't seem to need small talk any more than he did, and they walked together in comfortable silence. He had no sense where he was going, and there was no way to ask if she did.

The thing was, he realized, that he didn't give a damn, and not knowing filled him with a lightness he hadn't felt in as long as he could remember.

She was at home here; perhaps not from this valley, but from a place where the pleasure of walking a trail just to see where it led was reward enough for a day's labor.

He pointed out a condor wheeling far overhead, disappearing into the clouds that lingered over the park's sky-tearing peaks, and she placed her hand over her heart as if it were a blessing. Further down the path, she stooped to pick a weathered stone out of the river's bank and handed it to him; it was gray, with two thin white lines encircling its waist. She pointed to the lines and made a pantomime—a flock of birds? Snow falling? There was no way to know. He touched the stone to his chest to ask if he could keep it, and she smiled when he placed it in his pocket.

There, in Santino's, he pulled it out to show me. Fossils, he said. The shells of a million tiny creatures, settled to the bottom of the sea when this was all underwater. Crushed and covered with sand, pressed into a geological keepsake like leaves in the pages of a favorite book. That first thin line? That was fifty thousand years, crushed down to one thin line. The next line was half million years later. Two lines in a weathered stone to mark the unimaginable passage of time. He ran his thumb over the face of it pensively, then pocketed the stone and took another sip of his drink.

Their path ended where the river gave itself up into a lake on a broad gravel beach. She led him to edge of the water, a gentle lapping blue that seemed paler and brighter than the sky above them, and dipped her hands wordlessly, punctuating the destination. She waited briefly to see if he had any ritual of his own, then retreated a few steps and sat herself cross-legged on the ground against a piece of driftwood, looking out across the rippling expanse.

He sat beside her and studied the outline of her heavy, ruddy face. He felt a pang of sadness that she was not beautiful, but thought that the fact that she was not, and had always known she was not, had given her this inner strength, this unprepossessed confidence that let her attend to more important things. Here, he thought, was Hemingway's Pilar.

There were two rings on her right hand, simple bands carved of dark wood—ornaments, keepsakes. She was not married, nor would she be. He guessed she was somewhere in her thirties, at least a decade younger than him, but swarthy, already wearing lines on her face that a grandmother might. Chilean women might live damned near forever, but they married young, or not at all.

And here she was, alone, sitting on a gravel stream bed alongside a stranger with whom she could not even speak, eyes cast beatifically out to the horizon, out to the green and brown, to the gray and white layered on the far shore between two blues like the thin lines on the stone in his pocket.

He found himself wanting to take her hand, wanting to kiss her, there on rocky ground. She had connected to something in this place, and that connection gave her a strength, a beauty that, like Pilar, could blind a man to simple outward appearances while she held onto it.

She felt him watching her and turned to meet his gaze. It frightened him, this serene confidence, and at the same time he felt himself wanting to surrender to it, hoping that maybe she would kiss him, instead. Her smile blossomed at his apprehension, and she patted at the ground.

"Pachamama." She patted the ground again.

It was only the third, maybe fourth time she'd spoken, and the sound of her voice startled him out of the reverie. He looked at her blankly.

"Pachamama. Is Mother Earth."

He nodded, and seeing he understood, she went on.

"Pachamama is good...to us. Is good now." She pointed to the snow-capped ridge on the horizon, tracing its dips and spikes with her finger, then circled once at the sky above and again at the lake spread out below them. "I...love Pachamama." She thought a moment. "Pachamama...love me." Then she took another deep breath and leaned back against the wood, her sermon complete.

That was when he understood where her strength came from, he said.

"Did you sleep with her?"

"No." Jason swirled the remains of his Calafate carelessly. "We drank wine together that evening at the hostel. She recited Pablo Neruda to me and I read her Robert Frost. Neither of us understood a damned thing the other was saying, but the sound and rhythm of the words was enough. A Yankee craftsman and Latin lover giving meaning to the place where words are just sounds...."

He trailed off here in a way that left me uncertain whether he was talking about Neruda and Frost, or him and his mysterious Chilean. Or both. Honestly, I'd never known Jason to be such a poet himself and started wondering what other secrets he held. But I had broken the spell, and he was done for the night. He rapped the base of his empty glass against the table like a dismissing gavel and rolled himself forward to standing height.

"I'll see you back at the boat."

I told him I'd come too. Honestly, I felt kind of shitty for being so crass. We settled our tab, said our goodbyes to the kids on the couch and made our way to the door.

The dogs followed us down to the end of Boliviana, outside the guardhouse to the port. He said it again— that thing about love—after giving both a hug and a couple of farewell scritches behind the ear. Then they trotted off, satisfied with their payment, and we made our way down the pier in silence.

It was two weeks into the cruise, on the stretch from Clarence Island to the tip of the Peninsula, that Hank woke me up. It must have been around three in the morning: Jason was on the midnight-to-noon shift, and there'd been a CTD scheduled for about an hour ago. No one could figure out where he was, and Hank thought he might have headed back to his rack. But the top bunk was empty. Aft control? Ice tower? No, he'd checked all the obvious spots.

Captain had already turned the ship around by the time we found the note. We knew it was futile then: would be hard enough finding someone who'd gone overboard unintentionally, but without a float coat? Well, the shock would kill you long before drowning or hypothermia were concerns.

I took some heat from the Program for not reporting the conversation we'd had about jumping, but Captain came to my defense: everyone jokes about that, he said. Everyone.

They showed me the note. It was on a photo he must have taken with his cell phone, blown up to a grainy eight-and-a-half by eleven and printed in the ship's computer lab. I guess we'd all seen the photo before; he'd had it tacked to the wall-mounted wrench cabinet in the MT shed alongside the usual faded pinups, muscle cars and desert island fantasies.

But he'd written on the back of it: said he was sorry to inconvenience us, and he hoped we'd understand that this was what he had to do. That was all. And at the bottom, by itself, like an afterthought, he'd added this: All anyone's looking for is love.

They asked me to verify that it was his handwriting, asked me whether there was anything unusual about it. Whether were any signs that me might have been in distress, or "under the influence." No, Jason's scrawl was always that bad.

I still have that picture, and I take it out from time to time. It's pretty faded by now, but if the light's right, you can still make out the details. Halfway down a gravel beach, a swarthy, dark-haired woman in an orange sweater is turning to look over her shoulder at the camera. Behind her, disappearing into grainy, undersaturated pixels, you can see traces of green and brown, gray and white, layered on the far shore between two streaks of blue, like thin lines on a well-worn stone.

The Coal Creek Quarterly

The only thing that kept Sammy Waxman from sinking beneath the suffocating tide of failure was a short attention span. Sure, he'd been in and out of jail for petty larceny and mail fraud a couple of times. And that was after he'd watched every honest career he'd set out upon collapse at his feet for—to him— unfathomable reasons. But even before he'd finished wiping the dust off his face from the most recent bankruptcy or conviction, some gleaming thing down the road would catch his eye, and he'd be off again.

You certainly couldn't fault him for creativity. Take the Book Safe company: Sammy got hooked on the idea after watching a movie where the hero hid a chisel in his hollowed-out Bible. He started churning out his own book safes, buying discards from the downtown library and hollowing them out with a jigsaw in his brother's garage. They sold well on eBay, but the safes were only a loss leader. You see, Sammy understood that by selling a hollowed out copy of "The Arabian Nights" to John Smith on 453 Newberry Circle, you were inviting Mr. Smith to aggregate his most valuable portable property into one easily identified location.

The value of Sammy's client list was quickly recognized in certain circles, but law enforcement noticed a disturbing pattern in his online customer feedback. And while the plea bargain kept him from serving any serious time, it gave him a deeper roster of new enemies than most politicians can build in a lifetime of betrayal. He spent most of his year and a half at Coal County in the prison library; it was time to lie low and find a more harmless way to pay the rent.

It shouldn't surprise anyone that Sammy was a quick study, and he burned through the library's collection at a maniacal pace. The "self-improvement" section held nothing for him. It was filled with GED study guides and "Teach Yourself Spanish" books from the 60s. Philosophy, religion, technology, history—he read his way clockwise around the Dewey Decimal System searching for something to keep his brain occupied. Useless—every book was useless to him. The library's fiction collection was equally appalling. Everything, of course, had been thoroughly vetted by state librarians to meet the moral standards of the prison system. Nothing that conveyed even the faintest hint of unpunished turpitude could be admitted—who knows how it might lead these poor lambs astray?

In desperation, he turned to the periodicals, and was surprised at how the glossy magazines turned his stomach. The vapid obsession with celebrity gossip hadn't bothered him on the news stand, but somehow, here, under the stark fluorescent lights of the reading room, he couldn't even bear to have them in his line of sight.

Sammy pleaded with the librarian. "You've got to give me something to read. Anything!" He'd gotten himself so spun up tearing through the library's content that going cold turkey at the end was making him even more edgy and skittish than usual.

Cormack Feincastle was sympathetic—he liked to think of his part-time assignment in the library as a chance to do some of God's work, helping these men find redemption through reading. But he'd never found himself faced with someone as voracious as Sammy. He absentmindedly thumbed at the copy of *Rising Strong* on the table with pudgy fingers.

"Look, I can order more books. But all the business of getting requisitions and purchase orders—this stuff takes months."

"Well, what do you read? Can you bring books in?"

"You mean, like my own?"

"Sure! I'd love to borrow something. Anything. You know it's not like I'm going to run off with it."

Feincastle pondered the point. He did, as the saying went, know where Sammy lived.

"I...I suppose. What would you like?"

"Doesn't matter. You're a smart guy—I can tell that. What do you read?"

"I don't think you'd like it."

"Too racy? Too intellectual? Try me."

"No, it's...it's called 'literary fiction.'"

"Literary?"

"Yes."

"As opposed to what? Illiterate fiction?"

"No, as opposed to popular fiction. The mass-market stuff."

"Highbrow, then."

"I suppose."

"I'm game—try me."

When Sammy finished yard duty the next morning, he found that Feincastle had left a stack of assorted magazines on the library's carrel with a note: "For Sammy Waxman. Good luck."

He picked through the stack—an unnatural purple cover announced itself as *ZeitBang*; the slim *Northern Quarterly* below it sported a steel town-inspired cover page, and the ostensibly hip *Red Rock Review* looked as though someone had paid a lot of money to have it appear to have been assembled by kindergarteners. The contents of each looked remarkably similar: a half-dozen short stories, poems, an essay or two, always embellished with a liberal scattering of inscrutable illustrations throughout.

He spent two days trying to make sense of the genre, if that's what it was. The only common thread he could make out was that the authors took themselves way too seriously and appeared to actually believe that their rambling little stories exposed the fundamental nature of the human condition. That was a phrase he picked up from the masthead of the *Sandstone Review*: "Innovative fiction exposing the fundamental nature of the human condition." Right.

Sammy confronted Feincastle the third morning. "Look, I don't want to sound stupid, but these stories? They're not even stories."

"What do you mean?"

"A story is where something happens. You start out in a happy world and something goes wrong. Your hero tries to fix it and either rises to the occasion or fails tragically. The end. Either way, you've created some sort of dramatic tension and resolved it. But look at this crap: the guy's wife leaves him. He broods. He mopes. Then—ready for the big finish?—he buys an apple tree. And plants it. When I get to the end of one of these so-called stories I keep going 'Wait—what?' It's like I missed a page somewhere."

"Maybe it's a metaphor."

"For what? I mean really, Feincastle—you actually like this stuff?"

"I'm not sure if you're supposed to like it."

"So why do you read it?"

"It's literature. Good writing that..."

"...exposes the fundamental nature of the human condition?"

"Something like that."

"It's garbage. At least, in my uneducated opinion. My kid could write better than most of the stuff in these magazines."

"I didn't know you had a kid."

"I don't. At least, not that I'm aware of. Which is maybe my point. This stuff is painful and pointless. I don't see why anyone would want to read it, let alone write it."

"It's harder than it looks."

"Reading it? Trust me, I know."

"No, writing it. I've been trying to get a story published for something like three years now."

"In one of these rags?"

Feincastle composed himself. "In one of those journals, yes."

Sammy felt himself vaguely stumped. Feincastle seemed like a bright-enough man. Plump, pasty, and overly earnest, but at least bright. Why would he want to write crap like this?

He asked.

"I'm a writer. Trying to be one, at least. And these are the journals where all the good new writers get discovered."

"According to whom?"

Feincastle's hesitation triggered something in the back of Sammy's mind. It was a shiver of sorts, a spidey sense kind of tingle that tugged at an instinct he'd cultivated from his earliest days as a petty con in Minneapolis: there was a game here. And where there was a game, there was a rube, and a buck to be made off of him.

"Cormack," he said, in a voice that shone with newfound sincerity, "Mr. Feincastle. Please—tell me how this whole thing works."

The world of literary fiction was a revelation for Sammy. Here, he finally realized, were the ultimate suckers. He'd never been a writer; the best fiction he'd managed was the business plan for that alpaca farm in Bakersfield. But like any good businessman, he saw the opportunity for money to be extracted from the misery of others. Here was an audience with a desperate need for validation, any form of validation, and—more importantly—the financial wherewithal to pay for it. It was an opportunity he couldn't ignore.

It was obvious why people wrote this crap: they wanted to be loved, and they wanted to be recognized for the tortured, forgotten geniuses that they were. And they were willing to suffer—and pay—for that recognition. Suffering, in this case, meant churning out pages of angst-ridden emo prose in hopes that some literary fiction magazine, somewhere, anywhere, would publish it, thereby validating their existence. It didn't seem to matter which; they all seemed equally improbable. He browsed the bylines: "Joanna Birkson holds an MFA from Weston College and has published extensively in the *Weston Quarterly*, *Camphor*, and

BarfSplat. She is currently working on her second novel." Did any of these journals even exist? Sammy figured that the entire industry could be simulated by a couple of guys in a barn with a laptop and a good laser printer.

Here was the best part: these magazines had "reading fees" to be paid when you submitted. His survey of the back pages suggested that $15 was the sweet spot. The ostensible point was to provide a touch of monetary friction, to show that the author was serious about their piece (and who wasn't?). None of the magazines actually paid the authors they published—the putative fame and recognition was supposed to be enough. This was, or should be, a money mill.

Then there was the question of who actually read the published journals. As best as Sammy could figure, the answer was nobody. Or rather, nobody other than the poor schmucks who bought a copy in preparation for submitting their own heartbreaking work of staggering genius to its scrutiny. It was, open and shut, an opportunity too good to pass up.

There were some distinct disadvantages to arranging such a scam from prison: he would need confederates. Someone would have to set up the website—that was worth a little money up front. And he would need someone to handle the money—someone he could trust. That last part, given his traditional business model, narrowed the field considerably, but there were still a few old associates whose sense of mutual benefit he thought he could appeal to.

The hard part would be finding someone to do the actual editing. Sammy needed to find someone,

someone who actually cared, to wade through the anticipated onslaught of appalling manuscripts and craft the keenly-rendered "Sorry, but no." responses in a way that encouraged their desperate authors to try again. Someone naive enough to sincerely believe in what they were doing.

Feincastle was positively glowing.

"It's called *The Coal Creek Quarterly*," he said. "A breakaway literary journal"—he took a breath to make it clear that what followed was a direct quotation —"celebrating the best new voices in fiction."

Feincastle explained that they'd written to him out of the blue. They said that they—the editorial board— were rebels who had left posts at their stodgy old literary journal to form the *CCQ*. They were reaching out to promising authors whose prose had crossed their desk, but whom they'd been obliged by their nepotistic overlords to reject. Cormack Feincastle's name, they said, had come up independently several times; would he consider submitting some of his work for their inaugural issue?

Sammy looked over the printout that Feincastle thrust into his hands. It had only been three weeks since he'd set the wheels in motion, so he was struck by the degree of refinement evident in the digital letterhead; Dorothy was as sharp as ever. On a separate sheet, the one-page announcement of the *Quarterly's* debut and call for submissions read well too, propped up by an imaginary-but-impressive editorial board and hearty endorsements fabricated out of whole cloth.

The guidelines were familiar: 3000–5000 words, original work only, no poetry please. The normal reading fee would be $15, but subscribers had that fee waived for the first submission. The *Quarterly* would be pleased to offer an author discount of $35/year for subscriptions which, they hastened to point out, was "a substantial savings over the institutional rate."

Feincastle jabbed an eager, ink-stained finger at the announcement. "And here's the best part," he said. "Because they've read my work at their previous journals, they're waiving the fees for me."

Sammy was unstinting in his congratulations; it was easy to take honest pleasure in Feincastle's glee. Yes, it was just an elaborate ruse, but couldn't he say the same of the entire industry?

"But you'll still get a subscription, right? Maybe you could even see if there's budget to get one for the library, too." Honest pleasure or not, there was a bottom line to feed.

Dorothy Summerfelt had never considered Sam Waxman to be a friend. Sometimes a confidante, and sometimes a business associate of necessity. More often she regarded him as a thing to be pitied and stayed as clear of as practical. But his letter from prison had cryptically referred to her as his accountant, and requested that she come to Coal County Penitentiary during visiting hours to discuss his "retirement fund." It was only a two-hour drive from Anoka, and—damn him—he'd managed to pique her curiosity.

She had to admit that the scheme sounded foolproof, or at least low risk. And there was nothing patently illegal about her part of the venture. She knew nothing of literary journals, and had no reason to doubt her associate's information that half a dozen nobodies she'd never heard of were forming some sort of highbrow magazine. As far as she was concerned, she was a simple administrative assistant, forwarding requests and depositing checks when they arrived.

On the first round, manuscripts from Mr. Feincastle were to be responded to with enthusiasm; others, submitted according to website instructions, would receive the sympathetic cookie-cutter response urging patience: the journal, they must understand, had been deluged with enthusiastic authors, and its editors strived to give every submission the careful attention it deserved.

Once Feincastle had taken the bait, setting the hook was child's play.

"So—they liked your story?"

Feincastle's eyes were bugged out like a child at the head of Macy's line to sit on Santa's lap.

"Even better."

"How's better?"

"They've asked me to be an associate editor."

"An editor? What—instead of working here? We'll miss you, of course, but congratulations—it sounds like your dream job."

"No, no—I'd still work here. It'll be a volunteer thing. A few hours a week reading and recommending manuscripts they send me."

"A volunteer thing—you mean for free? So you work for them, and they don't pay you?" Sammy had crafted the wording of the offer himself during visiting hours with Dorothy the previous week. But he was worried that Feincastle, in his enthusiasm, had not grasped the nuances of the offer and wanted to make sure that there were no misunderstandings that could come back to bite him.

But Feincastle's fervor was undiminished. It was, he explained, part of the literary tradition. It was, he insisted, an honor.

"Well, then—congratulations to you."

Sammy paused strategically; it had to sound like an afterthought.

"You know...would you be in a position to let me have a look as some of these stories you're reading? I could help you out—be an assistant associate or something."

Feincastle's brow furrowed; his newfound prestige was still precarious. Sammy hesitated—maybe it was too early? No, there was a schedule to keep, and the clockwork was already in motion. He dropped the coup de grace.

"I mean, if this new journal really is all you say. I figure maybe I could learn a thing or two by helping. Might give me a better sense of purpose once I get out of here."

Feincastle went over like a five-day drunk. Sure— he'd appreciate the help. He'd do what he could to coach Sammy on the ways of reading literary fiction. Maybe, he mused, Sammy would even have a try at writing some fiction himself.

With the number of hours he was going to have to put in to get the site up and running, Terry Parker knew he'd get a better hourly wage at Taco Bell. But you didn't get the big jobs without a portfolio, and you didn't get a portfolio without spending a year or two taking lowball gigs on Dice.

Besides, the lady from Anoka explained, this wasn't just any literary magazine; it was a new, breakaway journal dedicated to celebrating the best new voices in fiction. The subversive nature of the project—and the chance to get in on the ground floor—appealed to him.

The best thing about this type of gig was that nobody had to know that Tinwhistle Studios was nothing more than a bumper-stickered MacBook Pro running a pirated copy of Adobe Dreamweaver. Nor that its chief (and only) designer was a creative writing major struggling through his sophomore year at Washington State University.

"They expect you to read fifty stories in your spare time?"

He'd told Dorothy to start Feincastle off small and wasn't prepared for the seven pound stack of paper Feincastle thumped proudly on the desk of the prison library. Clearly there had been some sort of misunderstanding.

"They're desperate - They say they've been overwhelmed by submissions."

Indeed they had. Dorothy confided that she'd simply thrown away most of the paper submissions after sending off terse but elegantly formatted letters acknowledging receipt of the manuscripts and begging for patience. The journal, they must understand, was still new, and had been overwhelmed by submissions.

She explained to Sammy during visiting hours the next Monday that they needed more help. The documents she'd sent Feincastle only represented candidates who, based on their cover letters, sounded naive enough to buy in, yet diligent enough to meet a quota. Perhaps Sammy could help Feincastle sift through them and get back to her with his personal recommendations?

The online submissions were an entirely different matter. Dorothy was sure there had been a mistake. She knew how these things went with computers: just one slip of the key, and suddenly you were charging the same person twenty-five times for the same thing.

Terry held the phone to his ear with a shoulder as he typed. No, he assured her, the SQL tables looked clean: there were 1437 distinct names and addresses in the database. Of those, 391 had purchased subscriptions; the remaining 1046 simply paid the reading fee for their uploaded manuscripts. He keened against the phone in the silence that followed. His ear for opportunity was borne of student loans and a diet of ramen, leftover pizza and peanut butter and jelly sandwiches. And the faint gasp in the silence that followed his calculation sounded distinctly like opportunity.

"You know, Mrs. Summerfelt, with this kind of volume I'd recommend you go with an online review management system. It wouldn't be that hard to add one."

It would be, actually, but he knew the money was there. And he knew, frankly, that without it, the newly-launched *Coal Creek Quarterly* would soon be coal dust.

"We could give you a discount on the standard Tinwhistle hourly rate, of course, what with you being an existing customer. But I'd have to check with my development team to see how soon we could fit this in."

He let the hook settle into the silence on the other end of the line. They couldn't say no, could they? Dorothy's voice, when she finally spoke, seemed far away.

"Yes...yes, of course." Score. "But...our editors can't possibly read that many submissions. Really—fourteen hundred, you said? How long would it take to read all of those?"

Her perplexity caught Terry by surprise. Didn't she know how all this worked? Wasn't she the big editor of this fabulous new journal? No, no, she confessed—she was just the administrative assistant. She was really a —there was an odd pause while she seemed to fumble for words—literature student. Her professor offered her the job if she could get everything set up for the editors behind the scenes. And—her confession gathered steam—she was in over her head, and she really needed this job. Was there any way he could help her?

Opportunity was ringing like a firehouse alarm in his ear. Yes, yes, of course he could help. He had some connections in academia who might be willing to lend a hand, might help recruit some qualified reviewers. Could he get back to her later in the day?

Of course Terry knew there was something fishy about Dorothy's story. But her $650 payment for the original site was real enough. They settled on a $5 per manuscript contract rate for referred submissions. Initially, Terry just skimmed the documents himself and entered a few choice comments in the recommendations field of the new system. The code had, in fact, come together quickly; he'd even added a section for Associate Editors and (with Dorothy's enthusiastic approval), installed himself as "Managing Editor" on the journal's online masthead. *CCQ's* executive team, she said, was eager to have his contributions properly recognized.

Eight months in, Sammy was getting nervous. He knew that in every scam there was a single optimal moment at which to cut bait and run. Too soon and you left money on the table; too late and you risked not putting enough distance between you and your mark when the game was up. Sammy suspected that there was a mathematical model for this somewhere, and that if he could just work it out, he could finally turn the corner and make something of his life. But math had never been his strong suit, and whenever a new opportunity looked him in the eye, the dollar signs seemed to hypnotize him; it never seemed soon enough to pull out until it was too late.

This time was going to be different. He'd worked it all out beforehand: these magazines promised a six-month turnaround time on submissions. He figured that sending rejection notices to most of the rubes— sorry, authors—four months in would give them something to think about and maximize the chances that they'd resubmit quickly in hopes of being included in the promised inaugural fall volume. That gave them nine full months to milk it. By the time Feincastle and now the upwards of two thousand other contributors began wondering what was up with their darling new publication, he'd be out of the clink and on his way. Dorothy would put up a notice announcing that, due to irreconcilable editorial differences, *The Coal Creek Quarterly* was shuttering publication. Refunds that never materialized would be promised for subscribers, while ordinary authors would be reminded of fine print indicating that the journal was unable to indemnify submission expenses. So he was a little taken aback when Dorothy showed him the lineup for the first online edition during their now bi-weekly visiting sessions.

"Our what?!?"

"It's to pump up our selectivity."

"What selectivity?"

"Acceptance rate. The lower your acceptance rate, the more selective you are. The more selective you are, the more people think you're something special. And the more submissions you get. It kind of feeds on itself. Like playing hard-to-get, you know?"

"Sure, I get it, I get it. But we're already at—wait, let me calculate this—zero percent acceptance. Right? You can't get more selective than that. If 'selectivity' was how it worked, we'd have goofballs lining up outside your door offering to sell us their kidney. Listen—this thing is a money mill. Why mess with it?"

Dorothy's nervous glance over at the visiting room guard suggested that maybe he was letting a little too much fervor seep into his reasoning. He let her speak.

"It's a PR thing, Sammy. Submissions from the original announcement are beginning to tail off. Print costs real money, takes months. But this online thing? It's like a dozen hours of time from the Tinwhistle guys, and we can have it out to our digital subscribers for free. Terry says it'll be like throwing raw meat into a feeding frenzy."

"Who's Terry?"

"Our Managing Editor. You know—the website guy, from Tinwhistle. He's got a whole staff of editors and reviewers lined up for the online stuff. And Cormack says that some of the stuff they've picked out is actually pretty good."

"Feincastle?"

"Yeah. I mean, I don't know. It all reads a little dainty and emotional for me, but Cormack says it's good. Good and... 'accessible'—that was the word he used: accessible. Anyhow, once the online edition goes out, Terry thinks our submission rate will go through the roof."

He shook his head.

"I don't like it."

"I appreciate your concern. I'll let you know how it goes."

It was only then that he noticed her body language: sitting back now, shoulders slightly askew, eyes resting on the spot where her restless fingers tapped at the layout sheet she'd placed on the table for him to see. That perfunctory impatience. No, she wasn't asking for his opinion. She wasn't seeking his approval. She was just, as a matter of courtesy, telling him how it was going to be, whether he liked it or not.

Sammy sputtered, searching for words, and she leaned forward again, honest sympathy in her eyes.

"Oh Sammy, don't worry—we wouldn't screw you out of anything. You're a full member of the board, and you'll be fairly compensated for your time and leadership." She bit symbolically at her lip. "But we've got this. And you have to admit that it's hard to be particularly...proactive while you're in here. We've had to make some decisions on our own."

Sammy found himself looking at her through squinted eyes. Was this the same Dorothy Summerfelt with whom he'd bilked half the pie-baking populace of Iowa out of $29.95 (plus shipping and handling) for no-stick, no-burn tins? She would never use a word like "proactive" on him, would she? And what was this about a board?

The inaugural edition of *The Coal Creek Quarterly* hit the post office to critical acclaim a week before Sammy's release. Feincastle brought in two copies—a subscription copy for the library and one, with the warden's approval, for Sammy.

"I explained how helpful you'd been when we were just getting started."

It was, he had to admit, an impressive bit of work: heavy bond paper almost half an inch thick, case bound, with an folksy but subtly hip rural landscape framing the cover. Sammy recognized none of the names on the editorial page except for Feincastle's.

"And you're a Contributing Editor now—no more mere 'associating' for you?"

Feincastle beamed with the guilty secret and put a finger to his lips. They were still working out the details, but he was hoping to cut back to part time at the prison in the coming months. The Quarterly had offered him a paid position that would allow him to spend more time honing his craft.

It took a moment for Feincastle to parse the vaguely lost look on Sammy's face.

"My writing. Working on my writing."

He'd noticed that, these days, Sammy appeared increasingly distracted and confused whenever he talked about the journal. He felt guilty about it. After all, Sammy had been the one who'd encouraged him and helped him in the first place. Helped him organize and wade through all those submissions in the early days. He'd been hoping it would rub off on his charge, hoping he could coax Sammy into the world of literary fiction. It would be a good creative outlet for all that obviously pent-up intellect.

"Really, you should try. At least give me a mailing address—somewhere I can send things after you get out, okay? I'd like to gift you a subscription. It's one of the perks of being," he paused for dramatic effect, "a Contributing Editor."

Sammy scribbled the number of a made-up Post Office box in Tulsa. "It's my sister's—she can get things to me."

"You wouldn't believe the coverage we're getting. Had to add two more full-time staff in Anoka, and the online edition's got, I don't know, tens of thousands of subscribers."

Feincastle's gaze had drifted away to the window, where the low autumn sun slanted in through dusty triple-reinforced glass.

"Next issue will be January, and we're already reading submissions for the spring. I'll have a short piece in both of them. I'd be curious to hear what you think, if you'd be willing to write me."

His stubby fingers pulled a pen from somewhere and inscribed *cormack@ccq.com* on the back cover of the magazine. He slid it back toward Sammy.

"Really, I'd love to stay in touch. I mean it."

"Sure, sure."

But the empty look in Sammy's eyes troubled him.

"Listen, Mr. Waxman—you're a smart guy. We both know you're much smarter than me. You've got a way with words. And I know you've got stories." He leaned forward. "I could help you, you know? Send me one of your ideas, a basic outline. I could help you turn it into something. It's what an editor does." He leaned back, gesturing magisterially at the *CCQ* copy still resting on the table with an upward-facing palm. "Really. I'd love to see a Sammy Waxman story in the Spring edition."

Sammy's laugh surprised him. It wasn't quite bitter, but there was a touch of something—resignation, maybe?

"Oh, I've got a story for you, Cormack. Boy have I got a story for you. But here's the thing: nobody would ever believe it."

The Slightest Trace of Gray

In the dream, he said, they'd met on a train. But had also always known each other; you know the way dreams are, right? I nodded, and he turned his head a little so as to look far away, remembering.

She had short dark hair, streaked with the slightest touch of gray. It somehow looked as if the wind were blowing against it, and there was a glow around her; she was a woman in soft focus and living color, biding her time in a charcoal sketch.

And this is where you met her?

In the dream?

Yes, in the dream.

We were sitting there, he said, pointing to the corner booth of the dining car. The booth had a long curved bench where four children of indeterminate age were squeezed in close to each other, turned outward on their knees, noisily distracting themselves out the long, low windows. Their parents sat mutely across the table, visibly grateful for the respite.

That booth, he said. The thought that went into designing that booth was one of the little touches that set the Coast Starlighter apart from all the other rail lines.

This is the only train with a booth like that?

It is.

I peered at him over my glasses, questioning, and he laughed.

Yeah, I know, it sounds crazy. But yes, I've ridden them all by now.

To find her.

Yeah, to find her.

We let the silence sink in for a minute or two, watching the early evening sun play against the train's shadow on the hillside, and I felt sleep creeping over me again. I had set myself up in the empty double seat behind him when I got on in San Jose. Five flights in four days just trying to make quota, chasing shadows that Higgs swore were good leads. I was just one quarter short of going up for review as senior rep.... But God, I was tired.

I'd barely settled in and pulled out the folder with the Sand Creek documents when he swung an arm over the seat back, turned sideways to face me and started talking, as though he was resuming a conversation we'd left off just a few minutes before. That was two hours ago.

The waitress interrupted our reverie to ask if either of us wanted another drink. I needed to drive once I got off in Paso Robles, and said so. He waved her off—maybe later; there was plenty of time left, and he needed to pace himself.

You never asked me why, he said, after we were alone again.

Why what?

You never asked me why I'm spending my life riding these damned trains looking for a woman who doesn't even exist.

Would you like me to ask?

Most people do.

He said the funny thing was that he hadn't even been on a train when he'd had the dream; he was in a hotel in San Francisco. Some acquisitions meeting, trying to get snatched up by Google before his little start-up ran out of money or was made irrelevant by someone else's browser plug-in.

One click can change your life.

I had no idea what he was talking about.

That was our tagline, he said. Stupid tagline, but we believed it at the time. It was so easy to believe things like that back then.

When he woke up that morning—no idea why housecleaning would be vacuuming out the room next door at six thirty—he couldn't focus. The memory of his dream kept coming back.

He tried to sleep on the flight home; maybe she'd come back to him then. But his engineering director wanted a debrief on what had gone wrong, on how they could spin this; maybe tell Facebook they were in talks with Google and hope to get sniped, and what pivots were left if they didn't.

That evening, lost at the dinner table over the inevitable how-did-your-meeting-go-Dears and did-you-bring-us-anything-Daddys, he just said Fine, and handed over the chocolate candy suckers he'd bought at the airport for precisely that reason.

He flew back to San Francisco a few weeks later, by himself, after his company had turned out the lights. Told his wife that he had some meetings, some connections he'd made on the first trip that could turn into job prospects. She seemed to know he was lying, but didn't question him.

She thought you were having an affair.

She never really asked.

Would you have told her if she had?

In the silence, I half expected him to turn the question around at me. A memory swirled, unbidden: flat morning light, and an unfamiliar phone ringing on the bedside table. But he was lost in his own recollections.

He booked himself into the Hyatt again, Room 322, facing the city. He'd moved the reservation back a couple of days to make sure he could get Room 322— the girl on the line seemed content to accept "nostalgia" as the reason for the special request. They got that all the time, she said.

He spent the day wandering the city, taking the ferry to Sausalito, and eating lunch in the terminal building. Ate dinner at Mills Plaza, just as he had on the first trip. He looked apologetic.

Kinda stupid, I know.

I'd seen people do worse.

For a dream?

I supposed that there were many different kinds of dreams.

Of course it didn't work. He dreamed about trying to catch a plane, about being stuck in molasses. About showing up at school without pants, and falling endlessly—the usual gamut you read about in self-help books diagnosing your anxieties. The same washed-out mess of dreams he'd had every night since that time he saw her.

The marriage lasted a few more months before they separated formally. It was as amicable an end as anyone could have asked for, especially given the circumstances.

I nodded in wordless recognition. It had only been a couple of years since Valerie and I had stepped back from that same abyss, even as it crumbled under our feet. And there were still days when I thought my time on the road was the only thing that let us hang on to the illusions that had drawn us together in the first place.

You know, he said, at first I didn't even know we were on a train.

Dreams are like that, I said.

No, even after the dream. I mean, you know how you remember things later, when something lines up?

I did.

He'd spent a couple of months exploring diners around the city, planting himself in corner booths, trying to remember whether this was the one he'd dreamed of, whether the window was right, whether the table looked the same. It wasn't until he saw an Amtrak ad that he recognized the curve of the glass, and remembered the way things had swayed slowly as they took a bend in the rails.

Once he remembered the window, he remembered they'd been on a train. He tried them all, until he found the Coast Starlight, and remembered the way the sun had looked on the water while they talked. Every time he rode, he remembered a little more: how she'd had a BLT and spun the cellophaned toothpick in her fingers while she spoke. How he'd ordered a Tab—he didn't know they still made Tab—and offered to pay for everything, but she'd said there was no need. The way she'd looked over her shoulder before getting up as the train slowed on the flat stretch into the station (he now knew that was Santa Maria) and had to balance herself against him. How she smelled like lavender.

A pair of bells sounded, and the conductor's muffled announcement—Paso Robles, next stop, would all disembarking passengers please blah blah blah—put a point on the conversation.

I guess this is you?

Yes, but I was traveling light; we had a little time yet.

You're getting off at Santa Maria?

Always.

And going right back?

Next northbound wasn't until morning.

We had another minute's meditation; the sun was almost down now and its flat light painted the interior of the car in slowing flashes of red and orange between industrial warehouses and the silhouette shadows of trees leading up to the station. I broke the silence:

How often do you do this?

Whenever I can. Usually once a week.

And you're going to keep at it until…?

Until I remember everything. Until I find her.

The brakes were squealing gently now; we were in the rail yard, riding the slow clatter of switches as platform lights drew abeam and came to rest in a sigh of locomotive relief. People were queuing in the aisle, and there was no more time for questions. There was a rental car to find, then a two-hour drive out to Sand Creek. And hell, I'd probably still end up sleeping in the car again.

I stood, and the forgotten folder spilled its zoning laws and contingency charts underfoot. I crouched to retrieve them, cursing absentmindedly.

Hey—he called to me, softly, as I wrestled my way into the queue of departing commuters. There are worse dreams to chase.

The crumpled sheaf of papers felt gritty against my fingers. Somewhere far off in the bustle, a cell phone rang, insistently. Yes, there are, I assured him. There certainly are.

Artifacts

It was pretty obvious that the girls thought I shouldn't have those bowls, and I wasn't at all sure they were wrong. They—the bowls—had arrived down at the Station under circumstances that weren't entirely official. Come to think of it, so had the girls. But the bowls arrived in a long wooden crate with some sort of machinery—honestly, could have been tractor parts—that came from Ushuaia. There were the official parts listed on the manifest, the usual dunnage, and then, stuffed in under some of the padding, the bowls. On some other planet, they could have been tractor parts, too—they reminded me of Navajo pottery, but looked like they'd been carved from spun metal instead of clay. Which maybe meant that they weren't bowls at all; I'd been meaning to look up the definition, if only so I could tell the story right.

Whatever they were, they were going to get chucked out on the berms once the folks from logistics got their parts out, so I took them. Put them on the shelf of my bunk, to brighten it up a bit. Put them next to the dreamcatcher my little girl had given me before I deployed out here. When the sun came around to my side of J95, it came in through the window and glinted. Threw the light around in tiny little spots on the green canvas, like stars in my own personal planetarium.

I missed the stars. Still missed getting them every night. Another month here at the South Pole and the sun would be gone, and then, of course, we'd have six months of stars, non-stop, and I'd miss the sun. Okay, closer to four and a half months; twilight on either end would make up the difference. But when telling people how things were here at the Pole, we always simplified it: six months of day, one sunset, then six months of night and a single sunrise. Repeat ad infinitum until the Herc comes and gets you for redeployment.

Anyhow—the bowls. I'd had them for a couple of months now, and they'd sort of become part of the background for me. There were three of them, one big and two little, and they'd nest if you slid them together just right. They had a dull finish, like old aluminum, and instead of painted decorations, there were swirling patterns cut out from the sides. A mountain with the sun behind it. Some lightning bolts, a man, and a stylized running bird whose tail stretched halfway around the midpoint of the largest one.

I'd had them up there on the shelf since—when was it?—oh, probably December. But no one had been in my bunk since then. Come to think of it, no one but me had been in my bunk since November, when Michelle left a bar of Kiwi chocolate she'd brought in from Scott Base on my pillow as a thank-you for fixing her computer. There weren't a lot of places to be alone on the station, so you tended to not mess with other peoples' bunks.

But there'd been some sort of problem with the cooling recirc in our pod, though—funny how even here you needed to have a cooling loop—and when the UTs fixed it, they knocked out a couple of overhead panels. So I filed a ticket for a carp to put the panels back in, and the carp brought the girls.

Still was strange to think of families living down here—I suppose it was strange to them, too. All part of the "new now", and we doing our best to, as they said "embrace the change." Anyhow, the girls were fine. I'm sure they had names, but they never spoke—well, almost, at least not to anyone except each other, and when they did, it was in their own language. Their mother had come from some small village along the spine of Patagonia, down with the most recent wave. She'd gotten work as a welder on one of the vessels—apparently she was phenomenal with metal—then made her way south until there wasn't anywhere farther to go. The girls came with her.

Somehow, when they got to Station, the girls latched onto L2 as a surrogate hen, and followed her around instead. L2—her real name was Laura, but down here, I guess we tend to lose hold of the names our parents gave us. When she'd shown up at the carp shop last season, we already had a Laura, also a carpenter, so for a while she was "Other Laura" or "Laura Two", before her name settled on its present two-letter form. It wasn't a big thing; I could think of half a dozen folks that I only knew by something their own mothers wouldn't recognize: Storm, Froggy, Mutt.

As I said, I'm sure the girls had names, but they just seemed like L2's unlikely adopted brood as they followed, and we all just called them "the girls." Straight black hair framing little round faces under their hand-knit chullos; I thought the older one couldn't be more than eight or nine. But I never was good at telling ages of mountain folk, and those wide dark eyes made theirs even harder to guess.

So L2 was standing on a ladder, poking her head up through where the broken ceiling panel was supposed to be, and the girls were bouncing on my bed, chattering at each other. They'd tumbled into my bunk when L2 had knocked—pushed past me and started sniffing and scouting every corner of my little six-by-eight wedge like puppies let off the leash.

"Sorry—do you mind?" She gestured toward the girls with an air of resignation, like there was nothing she could do about it. There probably wasn't.

"Nah, it's fine."

I didn't have anywhere better to be, so I watched as she set up the ladder and started poking around the ceiling. Watched her, watched them. I figured I ought to try and be a good host, and reached for the box of gumdrops I'd picked up from a beaker who'd left early in the season.

"Hey girls—want a gumdrop?"

They looked at me, briefly, with expressions you might find on the faces of zoo patrons who have just watched a seal bark, then resumed their play.

"Hey, here." I pulled one out and threw it. The elder one caught it, unwrapped the gooey blob and sniffed it, then handed it to her sister. She considered me again for a moment, trying to determine whether a second gumdrop would be coming, then turned back to the task of bouncing on the bed.

"Hey—there's another." She caught this one almost without looking, and stuffed it into a pocket in her dress.

I could have just left well enough alone, but this felt like a challenge and, well, Sundays were slow days. "Hey girls—let me show you something." I thought of the Navaho-like motif on the bowls, and reached up to where the top shelf hid them from below. There was a brief, high, piercing shriek.

When I looked back down, the two girls had pressed themselves flat against the plywood partition and slid as far away from me as they could, eyes fixed in something close to terror on the bowl in my hand. L2 had ducked her head back down from the overhead space and was crouched at the top of the ladder.

"Jesus, Karl—what the hell did you do?"

I looked back and forth between her and the girls.

"Nothing. Really. I just wanted to show them the bowls I saved from getting bermed last season."

"Well—don't. Christ, can't you see you're freaking them out?"

"I see, I see. But I don't know why they're freaking. They're just metal bowls I found. See?"

I held the smallest one up so she could examine it, and watched as the girls' eyes tracked it, the way you'd watch a snake moving through the grass.

"They're nice. Where did you get them? No, wait. Put them away. The girls are freaked."

I took the bowl back, moving slowly, smiling as reassuringly as I could as I nested the bowls inside each other, then lifted the stack to place it in the drawer at my feet. There was a brief stampede of small feet, and when I turned to look again, the girls had bolted.

L2 regarded me with interest. "Well, that was something."

I figured I'd track their mother down that evening to apologize for whatever it was I'd done. She was a day sleeper, though, welding on night shift, so she wouldn't be up until dinner. L2 had told me her name half a dozen times, but I couldn't ever get it right. Iqueta, she said, but all I could ever remember was "Equator"—I finally asked her to write it down. Yeah, I'd find Iqueta in the galley at dinner time.

But it was about half an hour later that Carter came knocking on my door. I don't think I'd ever seen Dan Carter out in the Jamesways of his own free will; like most of the station's senior management, he kept to the warmth of the station when he wasn't out in the field, or making his rounds. Carter's primary job was "physical security," which didn't involve theft and petty indiscretions as much as it involved preventing folks from hurting themselves or others in stupid ways. Someone nicked your boots from the locker room? He'd put a notice up on the bulletin board. Someone set up a jet-fuel-powered hibachi in the smokers lounge? Now that was his bread and butter.

So having Dan Carter at my door on a Sunday afternoon was cause for at least a little alarm.

"Here to check out the carp's handiwork? I've finally got something resembling a ceiling again."

"Sorry, Karl—this is business. I understand you've been keeping some sort of demon artifacts here?" He paused—it was a measured pause, calculated to gauge my surprise before continuing. "Yeah, that's what I thought. Sorry to bother you, but Iqueta came at me like you'd tried to feed her kids to the Rodwell. I mean, Megan was doing the translating—you know my Spanish is crap—but the gist was that you had some kind of machine or device here that was a danger to them. And the whole station, by the sound of it. You have any idea what she's talking about?"

I showed him the bowls and told him the story of how I'd ended up with them. He admitted he had no better idea of what they were than I did.

"You've checked that they're not radioactive?"

"Why would I have done that?"

"Mysterious metal objects showing up—who knows what they could be from?"

"They're out of a USAP crate shipped from Ushuaia. The entire continent's nuke-free—don't they check that sort of thing before they let stuff on board?"

"I suppose."

"Do you even have a Geiger counter? Does anyone here?"

"Point taken. But look—these things are freaking Iqueta out. Honestly, I think they're fine, and you're not doing anything to endanger anyone in the life and limb category. But wherever she comes from, they've probably got some pretty deep-rooted superstitions, and these things have snapped her mousetrap. You're well in your rights to keep them, but I'd take it as a kindness to Iqueta if you'd consider shipping them back home. Or at the very least telling her you were shipping them back home and making a good show of it. Could you do that for me?"

I said I would, and he said he owed me a beer for the favor and said goodbye.

I figured I'd still catch Iqueta at the galley and apologize for causing her kids grief. I could pick up a shipping box and some packing tape from cargo at the same time, and have the devil bowls on an outbound Herc by tomorrow afternoon. Shipping them to my brother in L.A. seemed like the obvious thing—not because of the "devil" thing, but because over the years his garage has ended up storing most of the useless crap I've acquired when it was no longer practical to drag around the world with me.

So I threw the bowls in my knapsack, stepped into my bunny boots and pushed out through the front door of J95. Iqueta was waiting for me there. Well, not quite "waiting"—more like "preparing." She'd carved deep gouges in the ice surrounding the entrance and filled them with bits of metal scrap. The effect was that of a miniature Nazca Lines painting—spirals and pictograms cut in a half-circle surrounding the door, brought into relief by handfuls of washers, bent wire and machine screws.

"You stop!" Her voice was authoritative, command-ing, with a raised palm outstretched like an old-fashioned policeman. She was a small, brown woman, with a heavy rope of thick black hair that she wore braided and tied back behind her, but she spoke with a conviction that stopped me in my tracks.

"Hey, sorry—I was meaning to come find you to apologize for the trouble. Carter told me, and I'm getting rid of the bowls." I knew she didn't speak English, but I had to say something, and was hoping my posture and conciliatory tone would get the message across.

"You stop!" She said it again, like a magic spell whose words had no meaning to her, but held someone's promise that, if uttered in the right tone, would produce the desired result.

"Yes, yes, I'm stopping. But I'm getting rid of the bowls. See? I've got them right here, in my bag." I patted the bag over my shoulder to add emphasis, and as I did, her eyes grew wide with terror. Her next "You stop!" was said not with a voice of authority, but almost screamed, loud enough that doors slammed open on J93, next door. A couple of husky firemen burst out at a run to stop what they could only assume was some violent assault.

I dropped the bag at my feet, arms outstretched. Her eyes followed the bag as it fell and the bowls emitted a muffled, bell-like clang when they hit the ground. By now Mike was between us, sizing me up as an unlikely assailant, but still using his fire chief's Command-and-Control voice.

"What's happening here? Karl?" He was in my face, ready to grab, tackle me—whatever was needed.

"It's okay! It's okay. It's…. Apparently I've got something in my bag that freaks her out. I was telling her that I was getting rid of it and, well, she freaked out."

"What is it?" But he didn't wait for an answer, and turned to where Jake was already trying to calm Iqueta, and assess whether there'd been any actual harm. That's when he looked down and saw the lines of metal drawn in the snow. He turned back to me. "What the…? Did you do this?"

"No… I… I've got these metal bowls I found. Carter told me they freaked Iqueta and her kids out, so I was going over to Station to get some boxes and ship them home. I came out the door, and she was here with all this…this ice voodoo and yelling at me to stop. Honest, I'm just as confused as you are."

Iqueta was talking fast to Jake, pantomiming a pushing motion directed at my dropped knapsack and the bowls it contained.

"Mike—you speak Spanish? I'm kinda limited here and she's going crazy fast."

None of us did, other than the usual "Una cerveza, por favor," so Mike called for someone in the now-assembled crowd to go find L2, Megan or someone who could translate. In the meantime, it became clear that it wasn't me that Iqueta had the problem with—it was whatever was in my bag. And as I stepped clear of the half-circle snow-drawing, she shook her head and gestured for me to go back. She wanted me to go back inside, to take the bowls and put them away.

Fine. I nodded in assent, scooped up the bag and retreated back into the darkness of J95. Once inside, I slid the drawer under my bed out, dumped the bowls away and pushed the drawer back in with my foot. I came out holding the bag up, open and empty, as though I was leaving the target of a police siege and wanted to assure the assembled SWAT team that I was carrying no armaments or explosives.

Someone had fetched Carter in the meantime, with Megan in tow. The rest of the crowd had mostly dispersed, but Iqueta still stood there like a defiant sentry at the edge of the carved rings, and the firefighters were absentmindedly digging the toes of their boots into the ice. Carter was still out of breath from running. He looked back and forth between me and Iqueta, sizing up the situation before speaking.

"Okay—it sounds like Operation Get Rid of the Devil Bowls didn't go as smoothly as I'd hoped. Anyone want to fill me in on what happened?"

Megan translated his question and Iqueta burst into a river of Spanish, gesturing wildly at me, at J95, and at the rings of ice and scrap metal at our feet. Mike raised his hand slowly, authoritatively for attention. He was a head taller than the rest of us, and even Iqueta stopped to give him the floor. He gave—in my view—a fair and measured account of what he'd seen, and assured Carter that the bowls were again secured in my bunk.

Megan raised her hand—it felt a little like we'd been called out by the principal for fighting on the playground—and gave her understanding of Iqueta's account. "She says that the bowls have demons, and that they can't be brought into the Station. She says they have to stay inside the circles here. That if they get out, they'll take her and her daughters."

Carter was intrigued. "She said that? The bowls will 'take her'? What does that mean? Why would they 'take' her? And where?"

Again Megan asked, then listened. "Because she left, no it's like left, but she's saying 'aterrizé' which is 'landed' or 'went down.' Her husband, or the village wherever—there are a lot of names I'm not getting. But she left, and someone wants to bring her back to wherever she came from." Iqueta pantomimed incomprehensibly, presumably acting out what she thought Megan was saying.

Carter put a hand to his forehead, slowly. "Oh god, so it's an HR issue too. Let's go find Linda. Mike, Jake? Thanks for the help—I think you can go. Megan, do you have a few minutes? At this point you've got more of the story than anyone else here."

We sat together in the upstairs conference room as Megan, Carter and I repeated what we knew. Iqueta nodded enthusiastically while Megan spoke. Linda's Spanish wasn't as good as Megan's, but it was good enough to ask Iqueta a few questions of her own. The gist seemed to be that the bowls were sent—or as Iqueta had it—"had come" to take her and her daughters back. That's why there were three of them: one big and two little ones. Now that the bowls had seen the girls, they knew they were there, and they were... a problem.

What could the bowls do? She didn't know, couldn't know exactly without seeing them, but they were metal, and it was metal and earth that gave them power. That's why she'd come to the ice in the first place when she ran away: the ice was a barrier that kept her people's magic away. She insisted that the bowls needed to go, but they couldn't come to the Station first—there was too much metal there, and they'd get loose. For now, they needed to stay where they were, out in the outskirts in J95.

Carter kept shaking his head in gentle disbelief—*the things I have to put up with*—but was willing to go along with any plan that would restore peace to the Station. We agreed that I'd bring some shipping materials back to my bunk and pack the bowls up there. We'd get Riley to print up a label for me and just guess the postage, and when the mail bag went out tomorrow morning, I'd meet her at the ramp as she handed everything over to the plane's loadmaster. No, no hazmat stickers, nothing fragile, just three metal bowls with bad juju that were causing a stink.

The sky was another bluebird day as Pole 57 landed the next morning, the first of probably six Hercules supply planes we were going to get today. I'd come down to the cargo ramp a little early—I liked watching the planes, and Carter had given me the equivalent of a hall pass for the morning. "Sorry Bill, I'm gonna be out for an hour or so—need to do something for Carter."

I felt the cold on my chin, and listened to the unearthly crackling of ice crystals forming in the air swirled up by the enormous plane's propellers as it pulled abeam of the cargo shed. I'd almost forgotten what I was there for when Riley drew up behind me on a Skidoo, dragging two green canvas bags behind her in the banana sled.

"Is that my special delivery?" she asked, pointing at the box at my feet.

"Ahyup."

"No liquids, hazardous materials, drugs, firearms or contraband?"

"Hey, if I had drugs, do you think I'd be getting rid of them?"

"Just gotta ask. I'm legally a postmaster on this godforsaken chunk of ice, so it's my ass in a can if you ship something bad. And frankly, I like my ass where it is."

I had no idea whether that was an invitation to comment, so I just put my hand over my heart and said, "I promise: no liquids, drugs, firearms or whatever else you said. Just three metal bowls."

"Okay—gimme here. See you tonight. I hear Baker John's making cheesecake for dessert."

From my desk down on the lower level of the Station I heard the Herc depart, the heavy thrumming of its four big engines resonating even through the thick walls. You couldn't hear them land, but there were three more departures that morning, and every time one left, I felt another light blanket of calm descend over me. The past 24 hours had been pretty rattling, and my dreams last night had been restless. The stick-figure man from the bowls, pulling at my arm, sliding flat, like a shadow across the walls of my bunk, watching me. The running bird, now flying, circling high over the snow, only it too was a shadow on my wall. I'd awoken exhausted, and had to unpack the bowls just to convince myself they were really still there.

The afternoon went quickly with menial tasks, and by the time we knocked off for dinner, I'd lost myself in the rhythm of tracing network cables and reconfiguring servers. I caught Riley in the galley as everyone was lining up for the bell.

"Hey, thanks for the help this morning with my mystery package. Good to have it out of here."

"Don't thank me yet. You didn't hear about the mechanical?"

"What mechanical?"

"Your Herc had a turbine failure on launch. Threw a blade. Turned around and set back down here. They're keeping it warm until MacTown can get parts and equipment delivered. Probably tomorrow, mid-afternoon."

"And the mail?"

"Don't worry. Offloaded everything and put it back in the mailroom. Federal procedure and all—can't let it be left unguarded."

"Wait—so it's in the station?!"

"Yeah—is that a problem?"

"Just… don't say anything to Iqueta, okay?"

"What, that your box didn't go out today? You've kind of lost me. What does she have to do with this—is it some sort of reverse birthday present?"

"It's… oh, I don't know. It's kind of complicated. It's a superstition thing. I promised her I wouldn't bring those bowls into the Station."

"Well, they're all locked up and impounded as federally-protected mail. It's not like anyone could get at them except me. And I'm not going to—remember that bit about my ass in a can?"

"Is there any way I can take the box back and keep it away from the Station? At Cargo, or my bunk until it's ready to go?"

"Legally? No."

"What if… okay—what if you happened to weigh the thing and discover that it had insufficient postage? And, like, I couldn't come up with the extra until tomorrow?"

"God, Karl, that's a stretch. Can't we just leave it be? It'll go out first thing tomorrow, and pretty much no one but you and me are ever going to have known—or cared—that it wasn't already gone."

I couldn't explain why it was important to me. Maybe it was the look in Iqueta's eyes when she saw me with the bowls. Maybe it was the dreams.

"Please?"

"Jesus. Okay. After dinner. After the cheesecake. Find me. And we'll go indulge in your little felony."

The air in the mail room had an acid tang, the scent of something not quite finished burning. The mail bag had spilled open as if slit, and there were scorch marks on the floor around a patch that looked like electricity had arced through.

"Shit, Karl—get the extinguisher! Is this your doing?"

I didn't think it was, and told her so as I grabbed the red metal CO_2 bottle. There was no obvious fire, at least, not anymore, but she called an alert on Comms, and firefighters were on their way. Pieces of mail had been singed, and Riley dug through the slit in the bag for the source. It was my box, blackened and cut through on one side as though someone had drawn thunderbolts on it with a flaming rod.

"Jesus, Karl. You promised!"

"They're just bowls, Riley! Carter looked at them— they're just metal bowls!"

By now Don was at the doorway in first responder gear with Jake, Billy and Freija behind him.

Riley looked up at them. "Thanks for coming, boys. I think we've got this, but I'd love it if you could stay with us."

Don advanced and knelt beside her. "Ah... maybe we should open that up for you. Billy—keep a bottle ready, okay?"

Billy stood to the side, nozzle aimed at the charred box. We backed away while Don lowered his face guard, slit the packing tape away and pulled open the lid. The bowls were still inside, still nested and undisturbed except for the shreds of burnt paper. They were cool to the touch as he lifted them clear and held them up for all to see. On the side of largest one were the etched patterns: cut into its side: the mountain with the sun behind it. The man and the thunderbolts. But now there was no running bird. In its place there was the etched drawing of a woman, long black hair tied behind her, with one hand up like a policeman, as if to say "Stop!"

Water on Travertine

The thing that bothered Benjamin most was that there was no way he would ever know. No way anyone would ever know.

Maybe it was quick; maybe his father never felt a thing: one moment he was lathering away in the shower, reveling in the steam-soaked reverberation of his best Neil Diamond, and the next he simply wasn't there. Dead before he hit the travertine mosaic that his mother said gave the bathroom a more Mediterranean feel.

Benjamin was seven when his mother had fallen in love with travel and with all things Mediterranean. The family had spent two weeks on a gulet, tracing the Turkish coast from Bodrum to Marmaris, and she went ashore at every chance in every backwater bay, intoxicated by the prospect of yet another unexcavated little ruin. She always returned, breathless with discovery, long after the rest of them had bored of their beach walks and water play and were impatient to move on. "Can you believe?" she'd say, "I think it used to be a Byzantine church!" She showed them a handful of penny-sized cut stones, onyx and turquoise. There had been traces of mosaic under the gravel, she said. Certainly beyond restoration, and it would have been a shame to let these strays be lost to the elements. The fragments now lived in a ceramic bowl on the breakfast table, mingled with other strays from her travels whose origins had been long forgotten.

Benjamin wondered for the first time what his father thought of the mosaic in the shower. He seemed to have gone along without complaint—or apparent enthusiasm—with most of his mother's home improvement projects, inattentively acquiescing to the slow transformation of the unremarkable Eichler on South Court into a sort of consulate-at-large for half a dozen competing visions of Shangri-la.

But what if it hadn't been quick? What if he'd lain there, knowing, bleeding against those tiles? What if he'd called out with the last of his strength, the last of his breath, and lay there waiting, hoping for the rescue that never came, until the water washed the last of his life away? Dr. Lazar had said you really couldn't tell, not with this kind of heart failure.

It had been about ten o'clock that Benjamin noticed the shower still running, and probably close to eleven before he began to think something might have been amiss about it. There'd been no school that day—teacher resource meetings or something—but he woke up at seven anyway and plugged into his Playstation, anticipating a full morning blissfully uninterrupted by responsibilities. Of course he had his headphones on—few things united his parents like an objection to the sounds of computerized carnage. But he got up at regular intervals: another bowl of Cap'n Crunch, another trip to the bathroom halfway down the batik-lined hallway.

It was almost noon when he called in through the open bedroom door: "Dad?" The shades were still down, and the Barong and Rangda woodcarvings that flanked his parents' bed loomed in the murk. A bright line of yellow radiated from beneath the door to the bath. He took tentative steps in toward it, stopped and listened for anything beyond the sound of running water. "Dad?"

He knocked, too quietly the first time, and then again, too loudly he thought. Then retreated to the kitchen and poured a third bowl of Cap'n Crunch. Not because he was hungry this time, but because it was something to do with his hands while he tried to think. If his mother were there... Oh yes, if his mother were there—but his mother had been there less and less.

There had never been any real animosity between his parents; the closest they got was when he found them standing across the counter from each other, shoulders tensed, choosing their words carefully so as to not be misunderstood. His father always looked at the floor, or closed his eyes and swayed gently during these conversations, as if afraid that eye contact with his mother would undermine his ability to think clearly. Which it well might have—she had a gaze, a beautiful, intense gaze that Benjamin imagined in younger days could have knocked the breath out of an unwary man.

Their words were always measured, respectful: "I'm sorry, I realize now that I must have misinterpreted your question. But do you see how it was reasonable for me to expect that all three of us would be involved in that decision?" And when the matter was resolved, they would return to their books in their respective corners: his father to the Wayfair rocking chair in the family room, and his mother to the Sumatran teak breakfast table at the kitchen's bay window. Benjamin understood that not all parents were so rational or considerate.

They spent more time apart as Benjamin grew older, his father retreating into his work at the lab, his mother venturing farther afield, to Bangladesh, to Burma, to Bhutan. She would be gone for a few weeks at a time, so by middle school, he was adept at most of the household tasks involved in getting himself up each day, fed and to school in clean clothes. Evenings, his father would join him on the couch, and they'd sit together wordlessly as one balanced spreadsheets and the other blasted monsters on an alien world. It wasn't a game of catch out in the backyard, but it was their own kind of intimacy, and for Benjamin it was enough.

His mother's return was always caught up in a whirlwind of excitement: new carvings, incense, silk scarves and breathless tales of sunrise at the roof of the world, or midnight rituals in a smoky village hut. "Oh, you would love Tarangire—the Maasai, the animals! I must take you some day," she always said. Benjamin noticed that she never seemed concerned with working out when that "some day" could be, and over time he came to accept her promises as something between an abstract declaration of love and a polite device for giving voice to her enthusiasm.

There was a deeper pattern of his mother's comings and goings, too. In the first days she was back, her volubility seemed matched only by the counterpoint of his father's silence. He would listen, and sometimes nod agreeably, but Benjamin observed that he rarely asked questions. And when he did, they were invariably for clarification rather than an attempt to delve any further into her story.

His father seemed to regain his own voice only after the storytelling days were expended and the family settled into a comfortable balance. It was, Benjamin thought, as though they only had one set of words between them, and the slow exchange formed a movement of the tides.

Benjamin's father referred to this middle period as "project time," and as the stories wound down, he and Benjamin would quietly begin betting which would re-emerge to physically manifest themselves on the household. Maybe a greenhouse, so she could grow salak? Or maybe a mandala? She had been obsessed with mandalas when she returned from Rajasthan. Benjamin guessed mandalas and basked in silent triumph at the dinner table when his mother announced that she had found one, woven exquisitely in Himalayan wool, to replace the living room rug.

In another few weeks, after the projects were done, the tide invariably ebbed to its other extreme, leaving his mother sullen and distracted. She would gaze out the kitchen window somewhere above the horizon, her dog-eared Jane Goodall forgotten among scattered Post Its, and seemed to only half hear when his father suggested that perhaps they plan for a Sunday afternoon drive out to the coast. Maybe they could hike up the bluff at Pillar Point? His mother would nod distractedly, but Benjamin knew that when Sunday came she would make some weary excuse and suggest they go on without her; he'd long since learned that cajoling her was futile. By the time she began packing for her next trip, she moved almost as a ghost through the house.

Benjamin finished the bowl of cereal, stalling. He took his time chasing down the last of the bloated, floating orange blobs, cornering them individually with his spoon and straining their grainy, cloying remains through his teeth before raising the bowl to his lips like a ritual chalice and draining the sugar-soaked milk. His gaze drifted down the hallway again; he really ought to do something.

Morocco—that's where his mother said she was going this time. "We'll be in Marrakesh for only a couple of days," she said. "Then we'll start working our way north, to the coast, and east, to Fes. That's where the real art is." The way she said "real" art struck him as odd. Also the way she always said "we," but never mentioned any traveling companions.

In any case, he couldn't call her. He couldn't call anyone, now that he thought about it. He had friends, and knew the neighbors well, but his mother was the only person on earth he could imagine stepping through the clutter of that darkened bedroom, rapping heavily on the door and announcing, "Hal? You there? I'm coming in," before doing just that, with no self-conscious hesitation.

He laid the bowl in the sink, then retrieved it and found an empty spot on the top rack of the dishwasher. Down the hallway, through the darkened bedroom, the shower hissed insistently.

Somewhere blocks away the moan of a fire engine rose, thickened and fell. Maybe someone else, somewhere else, had known something was wrong and had called for help in the meantime. He dismissed the thought as ridiculous and listened, two steps down the hallway, as the siren faded, attending to some other, more certain calamity.

Two more steps; now he was past the hallway bathroom with its wall of Senegalese masks, long dour faces and jutting lips. Benjamin always felt they were watching him, disapproving of his perfunctory toothbrushing. Or perhaps his mother had placed them there to discourage him from lingering on the toilet? Four more steps and he perched at the darkened threshold again. Then at the bathroom door; he placed his ear against it, listening, cursing silently to himself.

"Dad?" Only the muffled sound of water against stone. "Are you in there?" Nothing. "ARE YOU OKAY?" Nothing.

Jesus Christ. The air burbled at his lips—he couldn't get it to go down and make a proper breath in his lungs. His heart was beating, pounding. He placed his ear against the door again, a hand on the knob, turning it, trying it.

And then it was free from the latch, swinging inward, and he was bathed in light and sound and fogged mirrors and blue tile through the cold rattling mist of water on travertine, alone and with a question whose answer he would never know.

Wenatchee, Last July

I told Rocket that the girl at the fence reminded me of Bunny.

"Who?"

"Bunny. Kate. Katherine…what's-her-name. The stray from Louisiana. Weren't you with that part of the tour last year?"

She was standing alone, leaning gently with one hand laced through the chain link for support, watching the flat light of a waning day play across the planes out on the tarmac.

Rocket peered at her, squinting at the silhouette, and shook his head—no joy. He seemed unable to muster the energy to ask for more details; just out of reach, the cooler lay full of promise and cold Heineken, and it appeared to be winning out in the tug-of-war for his attention.

He waved a magisterial hand at Bobby, who'd just returned from wiping the last of the oil off the Mitchell's continually-bleeding left engine. It was the universal sign between men of a certain social class: get me a beer, willya?

Bobby fished one hand through the ice and passed a bottle to Rocket, then looked to me. Did I want one? Sure. I took it, thanked him, and dug into my pocket for an opener while he collapsed into the empty lawn chair between where Rocket and I sat.

It had been a long day. Then again, when the weather was good like this, it was always a long day.

We'd usually be pulling the chocks at dawn to get in as many flights as we could before we had to open the gates for general admission at ten. It was always a scramble to get everything back on the flight line, shut down, and wiped up pretty by then. Once the gates were open, we were on our feet until they closed again at five. And by then Ryan had usually managed to sell a few more rides; on good days we'd fly until sunset and put the planes away in the dark.

Not that I could complain. We were living a life most pilots didn't dare dream of, barnstorming our way around the country. In genuine World War Two bombers at that. We spent our days sharing living history with everyone from four-year-old kids bouncing on their moms' shoulders to the last of the old guys who actually flew these planes in the war. It was an honor. Rocket had been with the tour for…hell, he was old enough to have served when they were new. But it was Bobby's first year, and he was still picking up the lore where he could.

"Who's Bunny?"

The funny thing was that her real name wasn't even Kate. I was trying to recall how it all fit together, but I think Kate turned out to have been the name of her daughter. I remembered the look on the officer's face when he showed me the picture and I called her Kate; made me shudder a little.

It was early March when we picked her up during a three-day stop in Alexandria. Not Virginia—the one in Louisiana, about halfway upstate on the Red River. Usually we aimed for bigger towns: a bigger crowd and more rides meant more money to keep the planes flying. But the airport was an old Army Air Corp base and it seemed like the whole damned town had served active duty at some point; if nothing else, Alexandria was a matter of paying our respects.

Doesn't matter how big or small the town was, there was always a crowd waiting at the fence when we landed and taxied in. Big old planes like that, with half an acre of olive drab and big old round engines stacked on each wing, popping and burping history with every turn. There was always a crowd, and in the crowd there were always one or two true believers.

Most folks who came out would spend an hour or two with us before work or Saturday golf or spouse and kids obliged them to excuse themselves. But the true believers would be at the fence when we landed, and you'd see them there at the gate the next morning, too. You'd swap stories with them, show them around the planes and move on. You could see them out of the corner of your eye, circling around like a stray dog hoping for a bone; eventually, you'd get the question.

"Anything I can do to help out?"

It wasn't hard to be sympathetic. I remember what it was like on the outside, back before I joined up. For better or worse, we were the stuff of legends.

Still, I felt a bit like Tom Sawyer handing them a rag and asking if they could try to get at the oil around the left cowling on the Mitchell. That damned engine served as an ever-present reminder of the First Rule of Radials: if you're not leaking oil, you're out of it.

For the true believers, that rag represented a holy mission. Receiving it transformed them from a mere spectator, someone come out to pay their $12 and gawk, into a member of the brotherhood. Now they too were tending the sacred artifacts. Now they too had entered the inner circle.

Bunny was at the fence that afternoon when we landed in Alexandria. It had been a good flight up from Lafayette, trundling north over farmland on a glorious spring day. At 1500 feet, the carpet of southern Americana slipped past like an endless diorama: a riverboat making its way downstream, a farmer's tractor trailing dust, then stopping momentarily as the shadow of a B-17 slid across his half-plowed field.

I was flying right seat for Marley in the '17 that day. Taxiing us to the ramp kept his hands and feet busy, but once I'd gotten the cowl flaps open and boost pumps off after landing, my main job was sliding the window back and waving at the assembled crowd like we were big damned heroes.

I noticed her right away—sue me, but I always notice the pretty women right away. Small frame, sandy blonde hair with a sensible "farmer's wife" cut, in a knee-length floral skirt. She was right up against the fence in a clutch of maybe fifty others: ball-capped men in overalls, mothers trying to corral a restive brood underfoot, and the inevitable squadron of hunched and withered veterans, mounted on electric scooters and tended by their already graying offspring for one more chance to commune with relics from their long-faded past.

I chatted her up on the ramp once we'd cleared the backup at the gate. She was standing with her fingers clutched, about a wingspan back from the nose of the '17, contemplating it as you might a sleeping tiger at the zoo.

"You have a chance to climb around yet?"

She jumped a little, and I apologized for startling her. Then repeated the question. She had no idea what I was talking about.

"In the planes. Have you had a chance to climb around inside the planes?"

"You can...go inside?"

She was older than she'd looked from a distance. Ample crow's feet, and a sprinkling of ochre across her tanned cheeks. But still pretty in that old-time all-American way, with a small-town charm school smile grown comfortable in the fullness of age. And pert, slim—full of motion.

Her hands played a nervous game of here's-the-church-here's-the-steeple as we talked. The wedding ring was big, gaudy, cheap—I could tell even from here. So she wasn't one of those girls who came out looking to score a pilot for a night or two. Propriety aside, we tried to discourage each other from sampling the local wares, if only because it made sleeping arrangements awkward.

But no, she wore that ring like a shotgun over the shoulder; she wasn't here to sleep with anyone.

I walked her to the ladder at the forward hatch and coached her—go on, it's okay, grab onto the seat rails and pull yourself up—to a spot below the top turret where two people could stand side-by-side. We might as well have been standing in King Tut's tomb.

"It's okay—you can touch it. You can touch anything here."

By the time I'd walked her back through the radio room, along the bomb bay catwalk and around the ball turret into the rear section, she must've asked a million questions. What was this for? How did they do that? Were the kids who flew these planes in the war really just eighteen? She spoke like a schoolteacher, like someone who was used to asking and answering questions patiently, and she seemed obsessed with details I'd never noticed about the plane.

I handed her off to Charlie for a tour of the B-24 after we'd climbed out through the aft hatch. "Hey Charlie! Can you give...sorry, I don't think I got your name..."

"Kate."

I didn't catch it then, but now that I think back, there was just a moment's hesitation before she answered.

"Sure. Charlie—can you give Kate here a tour of the '24?"

Charlie's eyebrows arched appreciatively. Her back was already to me, so I pointed symbolically at my own ring finger and gave him an exaggerated "Ahem." I couldn't tell whether his shrugged shoulders meant "What a shame" or "When has that stopped me before?"

She was back the next morning when the gates opened, this time in jeans and a t-shirt. I was helping Zach replace a pushrod tube on the '25, but every time I looked over, she had someone at her side—Marley, Jim, Barry—pointing at the turbochargers or gear down lock mechanism. Or she was crouched beside one of the old vets who'd come out, beaming up at him like a kid during storytime.

By afternoon, Marley had her sliding around on a creeper, degreasing the belly of the '17.

"Hey - she asked what she could do to help, and I'm an old man. I can't do that kind of shit anymore."

We were flying out the next morning, two hours west to College Station. I thought she had come out to see us off, but she thumbed her flight sticker at me like it was a golden ticket from Willy Wonka, and flashed a triumphant grin: "I'm coming along."

We did take riders on transit flights, but they tended to be rare on legs like this. It was one thing to shell out a few hundred bucks for a half-hour hop around the neighborhood. But when you give someone a ride halfway across Texas, they need to find a way to get back on their own.

Barry told me she spent the entire flight up in the nose with her face plastered to the bubble window at the bombardier's station. We'd no sooner shut down than she was bouncing at the seat rails like a bunny, bubbling out half sentences of amazement. She kissed old Marley squarely on the lips when he stood up to face her, then her eyes went wide in mortification, and she clasped her cheeks, stepped back, and tripped on the base of the top turret.

"Oh, I'm so sorry—I didn't mean to do that! It's just... my goodness. Holy heaven above."

Marley waved it off like Yeah, don't worry—this happens all the time. But I'd never seen him blush like that before.

By the time I'd gotten everything secured in the cockpit, she was already up under the wing, wiping oil from the number two engine. I guess I didn't pay her any more attention until we'd gotten everything out of the bomb bay: crowd-line ropes, traffic cones, folding tables, and the dozen odd plastic storage bins of souvenirs we sold at the gate—you can fit a hell of a lot in the belly of a WWII bomber, and it takes a bit of hustle to get everything set up so you can let folks in for a look. But she was still scrubbing away when five o'clock rolled around and we cleared the crowd line for the evening flights.

"When are you heading back?"

There was a different kind of puzzle on her face. Different from two days earlier, when I'd asked her if she'd been in the planes yet. Her words came slowly, and from far away.

"Don't know if I am."

I didn't understand, and told her so.

"I figure I might stay a while." She was nodding, as though she were just doing that figuring right now.

"You mean in College Station?"

"I suppose."

She stuffed the tail of the rag in her back pocket and wiped a bead of sweat off her cheek. "How long are y'all gonna be here?"

Friday, I told her.

"Well, then. I guess I'll figure that out on Friday."

"Your family's okay with that?"

"Family?"

She caught me staring at her hands: The ring was gone.

"Oh—that." She shook her head again, this time more quickly, and seemed to blush just a touch. "That's just to keep the boys away." She patted the olive drab belly of the '17. "But I didn't want to scratch your baby's paint, you know."

Ryan was our ride coordinator back then. He had the gift of a carnival barker and could fill a plane like nobody's business.

"You did explain to her that this was a one-way ride, didn't you?"

He looked as if I'd accused him of stealing cookies from Girl Scouts. Of course he had.

"She said it wouldn't be a problem. I promise, those were her exact words: 'Oh, that won't be a problem.'"

Mary and Clara's room had a pull-out, so she stayed with them that first night; after that, Jim just booked an extra bed for her. There really wasn't any paperwork for volunteering with the tour, so from that point on she was just one of the gang. We all had the same deal: a shared room in the local Motel Six equivalent, a bag lunch of whatever the local coordinator dug up, and $20 per diem for dinner and incidental expenses. Someone somewhere back at HQ was undoubtedly doing the accounting, but out on the road, these things just flowed.

I think it was Charlie who started calling her Bunny, and she didn't seem to mind. "Quick as a rabbit, that girl is," he'd say, and she was. He looked positively offended when Jim shot him a sideways glance—"No, not like that, you pervert"—and for once I saw no reason to question his intentions.

Still, I don't think I ever saw her skive, not even on those days out in Stockton when the ramp must've been a hundred degrees. We'd all be hiding in what little shade we could find, and she'd be running fresh loads of t-shirts from the van, making change at the PX, or chasing down that wayward kid who'd snuck across the crowd line to get a closer look at the Mustang.

She never did talk much about herself over dinner, or when we gathered out on the patio for our almost nightly beers-and-bullshit sessions. She wasn't particularly evasive if you asked; you'd just find that, after a sentence or two, she'd managed to get you talking about yourself instead.

We lost her in Medford, about six months in. Jim said something at breakfast about how he'd gotten the strangest call. Someone trying to get ahold of Louise Osborne, from Alexandria.

"That's not you, is it?"

Bunny shook her head like it was the funniest thing she'd ever heard.

Jim said he'd gotten the man's number in any case. Said he promised to call back if he did run into her.

"Here it is, anyway. If you want." He slid the torn sheet of Best Western stationery across the table at her. She picked it up with an if-you-say-so grimace, looked at the number, shook her head, and stuffed the scrap in the same back pocket where she usually tailed an oil rag or two.

Last I saw of her was around noon, when she asked me to take over gate duty so she could "freshen up a bit." Jim didn't even have a cell number for her, so there was no one to call when we couldn't find her that evening. Clara tried the Best Western—maybe she'd not felt well, and had gotten a ride back? But there was no answer in the room, and the kid at the desk couldn't recall having seen anyone matching her description since morning.

* * *

It was in Wenatchee that Agent Harvey came out to the airport to see us. FBI, Missing Persons Bureau, he said, and showed us his badge. He'd spoken with—he flipped through a spiral-top notepad—a gentleman named James Davidson a couple of weeks earlier.

Jim nodded silently.

Mr. Harvey was seeking information on a Mrs. Louise Osborne, and was hoping we might be able to help him establish her whereabouts.

"'Mrs.,' you said?"

"You know her?"

We glanced at each other in the circle that had formed around him. Mr. Harvey looked less like my impression of an FBI agent than an insurance adjuster called away from his desk. He was weary and uncomfortable in noonday sun. But there was an earnest look in his eyes.

Charlie answered for us all. "Don't think so. Is she in some kind of trouble?"

"I hope not. But her husband is worried about her."

"Where's her husband?"

"Alexandria. The one in Louisiana, not Virginia."

We nodded knowingly, but said nothing. Mr. Harvey took this as his cue to elaborate.

"It seems Mrs. Osborne had been out to see your aircraft when you were in town a few months back. And disappeared shortly after. I was hoping one of you might be able to recognize her from photographs. Maybe tell us whether you'd seen her that day. Maybe whether you remember anything that could help us find out what might have become of her."

He pulled an eight-by-ten collage of printed photos from a manila envelope and we passed them around, pretending to examine them with interest. Of course we knew who she was. The question was what we were going to tell him.

In the end it was Jim who owned up to it. Yes, we'd seen her. She'd traveled with us for a bit and seemed to have left of her own free will. He wasn't familiar with her situation at home, he said, so he wasn't sure he felt obliged to help the Bureau track her down more than that.

"I might need check with the Foundation's lawyers before we discuss this any further."

Agent Harvey shook his head as if taking off a heavy overcoat.

"No—no need for that. She's certainly of legal age and not under any criminal investigation." His expression seemed to soften, and something came alive in him as he spoke. "As long as we have credible evidence that no foul play was involved, which I think we now do, then, well...." He looked out across the tarmac, seeming to take in the magnificence of the July afternoon for the first time.

He shrugged. "I think we're done here."

We gave him a tour of the planes before he left, and he bought a B-17 cap on the way out. I walked him back to the parking lot.

"You said she called herself Kate?"

"She did," I told him.

"She had a daughter named Kate. Lost her to pneumonia, I understand. Late last year."

"Any other kids?"

He shook his head. "Only a pain-in-the-ass husband who says he'll teach her a thing or two when she gets back."

We walked the rest of the way in silence.

"You think she'll ever go back?"

He laughed. "I hope the hell not."

He fumbled for the keys of his rental car, unlocked the door and settled into the seat, then looked back up at me.

"Understand that you're not obliged to tell me, but you really don't have any way of getting in touch with her?"

I shook my head, and he nodded with the quiet resignation of a salaried government employee. Just doing his job and had to ask. But his eyes darted a moment and met mine with an afterthought.

"Pity. But listen—if you do happen to run across her again?"

"Yeah?"

"Do me a favor: Tell her good luck out there."

I promised I would. He pulled the door shut, started the engine up and clattered off slowly in loose rock and dust.

I was kind of relieved that we didn't stop in Alexandria the next year; not sure what I would have said if she'd come out to meet us there. But I was hoping, somehow, that we'd see her somewhere along the tour. Maybe not Medford, but somewhere.

Bobby squinted toward the fence.

"You think that might be her?"

No, definitely not. Just reminded me of her in a way.

"But tell ya what, Bobby—do me a favor: wander on over there and say howdy, will ya? See if maybe she'd like to come over and have a look at the planes."

Eight in Three Weeks

Seems like it rained fire ants all afternoon that day. They dripped from the gutters on the old cedar-shingled house and drizzled from the leaves of the sycamore that stood a little farther up the mossy rise. Sometimes they just seemed to fall from the clear Missouri sky itself.

I was seven—eight in three weeks, I was eager to inform anyone who asked—and we were halfway from Denver to Pittsburgh in The Beast. That's what my father called the hulking Chevy Impala we were driving east on an improvised roadtrip to see my great Uncle Walter. Walter was not doing so well, and my father felt some obligation to, as they said, pay his respects. But I gathered that old Walt wasn't in imminent danger of kicking the bucket so, weighing the expense of flying, my father figured he'd use the drive as an opportunity to take care of some business along the way. My father was all about opportunities to "take care of some business."

"Any chance you'd be willing to take Paul?" My mother was also alert to opportunities, and apparently I'd been enough underfoot that summer that she was eager to have me out of the house. I don't suppose I could have blamed her—seven-going-on-eight and fueled by Pepsi, beef jerky, and Roadrunner cartoons might make a boy tiresome after a while.

My first taste of Interstate 70 eastbound was a near-religious experience, with straight line roads leading off to infinity under an impossibly big sky. Summer trips had always been to the west, into the mountains at Estes Park, and the revelation that the world could be so large and wide open kept my face plastered to the passenger side window halfway through Kansas. We stopped every couple of hours, filling up on gas when we needed a bathroom break and buying burgers, milkshakes, and fries whenever my dad saw a White Castle. "You know, you can't get these back in Denver," he'd say, and hold one of the steam-cooked little squares aloft like he was eyeing a precious gem in the sun.

We pressed on to Sedalia that first day, arriving after dark at a Super 8 Motel on the west side of town. My father set me on the bed in front of the TV and told me he "had some business to attend to," but that he'd be back before too long, and I should stay out of trouble. I flipped through the channels—CBS, ABC, NBC, and a ghost of some local program coming in from Kansas City, then gave up and turned my attention to the Silver Surfer comic I'd negotiated for at a Sinclair station in Topeka.

I have a vague recollection of being gently lifted from where I lay sleeping and tucked into bed that night. I must have gone in face down, because my comic book was wrinkled and smeared in the morning, and my left cheek bore incriminating blue and yellow ink splotches matching the ruined page where Calizuma had pinned Norin Radd in a crystal energy sphere.

Whatever business my father had attended to must have gone well: he was whistling up a storm as we pulled from US 65 onto the wide open Interstate that morning. "We've got an easy day ahead of us, Paulie—an easy day," he said, drumming the steering wheel. I didn't respond—I was preoccupied with figuring how I might puppydog that good mood into a new Daredevil comic at the next rest stop. But my father said we didn't have far to go and we had all day to get there. There was more business that evening in St. Louis, only a three-hour drive away. And between here and there, he said, lived an old friend of his, an old friend he was looking forward to introducing me to.

It close to noon when we pulled up a dirt road that matched the hand-drawn map my father had scrawled on a White Castle napkin some time the previous day. The road snaked a short way into the woods, then dissipated into a clearing at the river's edge, revealing a tired gray homestead balanced on uneven land. The old house was missing so many shingles that it looked like a giant punch card, lumber poked through a gaping hole in a derelict barn, and what would have passed for a lawn was a thick carpet of moss that grew mounded in places, leaving hints of engine blocks, car tires and yard machinery that had been left too long in one spot. Behind the house, a stone's throw up the rise, stood a magnificent sycamore that cast the yard beneath it in seemingly perpetual shadow.

"Stumpy? Stumpy—is that you?" A broad-shouldered hulk of a man slapped the screen door away and stamped, heavy-footed, out onto the narrow porch and down the steps to meet us. I was puzzled at first—I'd never heard anyone call my father "Stumpy"; I don't think I'd ever heard anyone call him anything but "Steve" or "Dad" or—in the case of my mother, "Dearest". But my father swung out of the car and embraced the enormous stranger, his head barely clearing the man's shoulders; I'd never seen him look so small by comparison.

"Mott—what the hell?!? What's Molly been feeding you?"

The man coaxed an unkempt handful of black hair back from his unshaven face and corralled it with a Wilson Feeds baseball cap. He gave a small snort.

"Nah, Molly's been gone almost a year. Houston, with some artsy-ass writer."

"The bitch!"

I'd never heard my father swear, and in the shock of it I failed to clear the Impala's door as I swung it shut —the lower rail caught my knee and took me down like a rag doll.

"No, no—Molly's a good woman. She did right. Just never did learn that you can't change a man."

My sudden disappearance behind the car had caught Mott's attention. "That's right—you said you were bringing your boy with you! Jesus—a little Stumper—who'd have thought?" He paused in his conversation to peer across the car's roof, to where I was trying to recover my dignity. "You okay, little guy?"

My father introduced me, Paul Slocum, seven years old—"Eight in three weeks," I corrected him—and his ostensible pride and joy. I stood as straight as I could and held out my palm to shake hands with the giant.

"Paulie—this is Mott. He saved my life a couple of times when we were younger. Bravest, kindest, craziest man you'll ever meet."

Mott rocked his head from side to side as he stooped to engulf my hand in his. "Your dad's being overly kind there, young man. But that's his way, as you know." I didn't, not particularly, but thought better of asking for clarification.

"So Paulie—you okay with 'Paulie'? Or do you prefer 'Paul'?" I nodded yes, then no as he went on. "You eaten yet? I was about fix up some lunch."

I gaped at the sheer scale of the man as we followed him up the porch and into the kitchen. I pictured him a walking tree, an ancient colossal scarecrow made of redwood trunks with shoulders draped in old checkered flannel on which pteranodons could perch unnoticed, like finches. In the imperfect camera of my mind, I remember moss hanging from his arms.

But it was with light and practiced feet that he stepped over and between the cardboard boxes, empty jars and broken appliances that littered the kitchen floor. "Stumpy—you grab a couple three plates from the sink and rinse 'em up? I got some Ozark honey a friend brought me a week or two back. We can use for sandwiches."

I didn't have the words for it, but I could tell that my father's relationship with this man was something I'd never seen before. Mott's words had the sound of a suggestion but the weight of an order—a polite order, amiably given, but an order nonetheless—and there was a curious eagerness with which my father complied. When I'd seen him follow orders before it was always with the sullen defiance of a beaten man— orders from the man at the agency, from the lawyer, from the policeman. This was something different, and it fascinated me how my father fell into the habit of following Mott as easily as Mott fell into the habit of leading him.

That day was the first I'd heard of peanut butter and honey sandwiches, and the smell of warm honey still brings me back to the way the light slanted through those dirty kitchen windows. But my attention waned once the sandwiches were eaten and my second tall glass of lemonade finished; Mott seemed to understand this and gave me leave to explore the property while he and my father caught up. My father threw a perfunctory "Don't you get into any trouble, Paulie," warning after me as I trotted down the decaying porch steps, and Mott's voice followed his indistinctly, the only discernible part being "fire ants."

I found the anthill in question a little beyond the end of the dirt driveway. I'd heard of fire ants, and as a naturally curious almost-eight-year-old, I sought out a stick with which to poke the unsuspecting colony. The ants responded vigorously enough to convince me to drop the stick, and I watched a littler longer from a safe distance before retreating to the car for my Silver Surfer—the Esso station we'd stopped at in Jonesburg had had no comics to speak of.

The afternoon sun had made the Impala's vinyl bench seat unbearable, and after trying and discarding a few other locations (under the sycamore—too scratchy, against the barn—spiders), I settled in on the porch steps, where snatches of conversation from inside came through the screen door.

"...And you'll never guess..." "No shit? Is she still all or nothing?" "Seeing as I told him twice that dog won't hunt...."

I found myself drawn in, forgetting my comic book and trying to follow the stories being swapped inside the kitchen. Here, for the first time, I had a window into a forbidden world, a world of men unfettered by the niceties and constraints of family life. Their voices felt authentic—honest and unguarded, not like the stilted exchanges of adults when they knew there were children nearby, or the impossibly-contrived TV conversations of Mary Tyler Moore, or All in the Family. No, this, I understood, was how men really talked.

I inched closer to the door, trying to hear better, but the creaking timbers gave me away.

"Paulie—is that you? You find them ants?"

I stood and presented myself at the door, trying unconvincingly to look like I had just come up the stairs that moment, but Mott waved me in like an old friend newly come to the party, and my father did not object. I realized that I'd left Mott's second question unanswered and piped in a hearty "Yes, sir." I don't know where the "sir" came from—I'm not sure I'd ever used that word before. But there was something I heard in my father's voice, something that made it the only natural way to address this improbable man.

"Yup, I've been meaning to fix them for a couple of times now. Came up this spring, and you can't poison them out and you can't drown them out. Pretty much all you can do is burn them out—fight fire with fire, like they say."

"That's what I hear." This was my father.

"But this one, I've already tried burning them. Most of a gallon of gas down that hole and lit it up. Burnt for something like 15 minutes, it did, and you could feel heat on the ground ten feet away. But they were back, I don't know, less than a month later, right same spot."

My father whispered, "Damn."

"So here's what I figure: those bastards built such a maze of tunnels that you can't never smoke them out. It's like Cu Chi all over again—hell, they're even red, just like the Cong."

My presence seemed to have been forgotten by this point, and the two men were lost in their communion.

Mott drew himself up in the seat. "But we've faced this before, haven't we, Corporal Stumpy? And what do you do if you can't smoke a tunnel?"

My father looked dubious. "You gonna crimp them? With what—fire crackers?"

The smile on Mott's face grew slowly, deliberately, like he was waiting to deliver the punch line of a joke. "Come with me—yeah, we should do this right now. Oh Paulie, you'll like this." The big man rolled forward onto his feet and stood, rising so suddenly that it felt as though he had just materialized there, then turned and trotted out the screen door without waiting to see if we would follow.

"Dynamite? Jesus, Mott—you just keep this lying around?"

My father cradled the greasy brown paper cylinder the way I imagined one might hold a newly caught fish —delicately, to avoid crushing it, but firmly enough to prevent it from getting away if it should try to jump.

"Oh, we've got plenty interesting things from down the quarry. They always give you five sticks for a job you can do with three, and there's no point in wasting, is there? This ain't the good stuff, though, but it'll pack right, I reckon."

I was transfixed. For any boy like me, whose Saturday mornings had been so effectively defined by Looney Tunes, dynamite was as mythical a creation as Bugs Bunny and Road Runner, existing only in the colorful world of a glowing cathode ray tube. It was the bright red bundle with a sputtering fuse that served as the inevitable punchline for any of Wile E. Coyote's doomed schemes. And yet here it was, impossibly mundane, resting in my father's visibly quivering hands.

Mott read my fascination with obvious approval. "Go on, Paulie—you can touch it. If your father says it's okay, that is. And don't you worry—it's not all that bad. Not unless you let it get old, and the nitro sweats out. Then you get the crystals, and you can't even fish with it."

"You fish with this stuff?"

"Main reason to keep it around. I mean, it's not sporting, but sometimes you get the end of a bad day and you need something to show for dinner, right?"

"Jesus."

I could tell that Mott was enjoying this. "Go on, Paulie. You don't mind, do you, Slocum? Just hold it there so your boy can touch it." My father wasn't sure whether he did mind or not, but Mott had done that thing with his voice again—the order that didn't sound like an order—and my father turned to let me approach the magical, terrible artifact. His own voice was paternal and supportive, but flushed with uncertainty.

"Okay, here you go. Just two fingers, gently, right there on top. Yes, just like that."

"Two fingers" was how we'd been taught to pet rabbits, or to feel the grain on an expensive piece of furniture my parents wanted us to appreciate.

I was surprised at how shabby the stick looked, thinking that at least someone could have used better paper to wrap it. There were old, stained numbers printed on the side, the words "DANGER" and "MFG. BITMAG CRP." in faded gray, and improbably, an American flag. I rubbed my fingers together after touching it, fascinated with the oily residue the paper had left on them.

"Ahyup, that's the nitro just starting to sweat. It's no harm, not like that. But that's why we're using this one 'stead of the others. Anyhow—let's set that down and go dig ourselves a hole, right?"

In the time it took my father to gingerly replace the dynamite back in its burlap-lined crate, Mott had gone around the back of the barn and returned with a post hole digger.

"A'course, we need to discourage them bothering us while we dig. Paulie—you go fetch me the can of hairspray above the sink, will you?" I ran to comply, wondering what a man like this would be doing with hair spray.

When I returned with the unlikely can of Afro Sheen, Mott and my father were surveying the fire ants from a distance of about five feet. Mott shook the can, aimed it at the mound and casually flicked the lighter he'd produced from his back pocket. A curtain of flame erupted from the spray cap and bathed the ground, singeing the grass in its path and producing an acrid black smoke.

"There, that ought to get us started. Stumpy, you're on flamethrower duty. Keep your fire on the metal part of the digger—rather not have them coming out to fight. Paulie? You might just stand back a touch." I needed no more encouragement to back further away.

My father took the Afro Sheen and lighter and, following Mott's direction, concentrated its fire on the center of the mound for the time it took Mott to plant the twin scoops of the digger and wrench out a foot-long cylindrical section of earth.

"That looks good. Paulie—you want to go fetch the dynamite?"

I didn't know if that was a test, and if it was, whether his purpose was to test me or my father, but my father answered first. "I'll get it, Paulie—you stay here with Mott."

He returned, swinging the stick—but gently—in one hand as he walked, trying with minimal success to exude an air of casual comfort. Mott took it and eyeballed the hole, which was now teeming with angry fire ants.

"I guess I didn't figure this one all the way to the end, gentlemen. I was counting on being able to set this and plug it, but we're not going to be able to do that without your dad keeping them under the fire. Which I don't reckon is the best circumstance for working with dynamite." He sank to the ground in a squat, fingers combing the stubble on his chin. After a few seconds he rose with new determination.

"Okay, here's what we're doing. Stumpy, you clear that hole with the spray, then back off. I'll put the stick in and we'll tamp it with the plug I pulled. Paulie? You might best step back a bit further." But I was frozen in fascination, mesmerized by the atmosphere of danger and the story playing out before my eyes. I could see this man in the jungles of Vietnam, under fire, giving orders to his troops. They needed a plan, and Sergeant Mott was going to come up with one. And now I saw my father there too—brave in a way I'd never imagined, trusting, and willing to do what needed to be done.

"Paulie?"

"Yes sir?"

"You heard what the man said. Best back off a little ways."

I complied and retreated to a spot behind the sycamore, where I peered out sideways, like a small child playing hide-and-seek.

"You ready, Stumpy?"

"Yes sir."

"Okay, light 'er up and sweep it a little."

Flame erupted again from the can, and I could feel its warmth on my face.

"Okay—that's good. Flame off, I'm coming in with the charge."

Mott advanced with the greasy stick of dynamite, placed it upright in the hole with one deliberate action and turned to fetch the plug of earth from the post hole digger.

My best guess is that it was an ember of burnt grass that hadn't quite gone out, but Mott was two steps away when my father's voice rang out with an urgency that still remains with me.

"Jesus—fire in the hole! Live charge!"

Mott didn't even turn to look—he took off running in the direction he was facing. My father was running too, toward me and the protection of the sycamore. He rounded the corner in five steps and pulled me—still gawking stupidly at the smoldering hold—beside him against the lee side of the trunk. Then there was a sound like timber splitting, and the sky turned dark with brown Missouri dirt.

About the Author

David Pablo Cohn draws his stories from first-hand experience working at Silicon Valley startups, at the Amundsen-Scott South Pole Station, on Antarctic icebreakers and as an international election observer in rural Africa. He holds a Ph.D in Computer Science and is a certificated flight instructor specializing in antique aircraft. His novella, *Heller's Tale*, appeared in 2016, earning praise for its gripping and detailed depiction of life "on the Ice." His non-fiction has been published in such diverse venues as *Flight Training Magazine*, *The Paris Review Daily*, and *The Journal of Artificial Intelligence Research*.

David Pablo Cohn's writing and travels online can be found at http://davidpablocohn.com

About Montemayor Press

Montemayor Press is an independent publisher of literature for children and adults. To learn more about our books, visit

www.MontemayorPress.com

or write for a catalogue at:

Montemayor Press
P. O. Box 546
Montpelier, VT 05601

CPSIA information can be obtained
at www.ICGtesting.com
Printed in the USA
FSOW04n0417040617
34729FS